The Imperfect Lyon

The Lyon's Den Connected World

Aviva Orr

© Copyright 2025 by Aviva Orr
Text by Aviva Orr
Cover by Dar Albert

Dragonblade Publishing, Inc. is an imprint of Kathryn Le Veque Novels, Inc.
P.O. Box 23
Moreno Valley, CA 92556
ceo@dragonbladepublishing.com

Produced in the United States of America

First Edition January 2025
Print Edition

Reproduction of any kind except where it pertains to short quotes in relation to advertising or promotion is strictly prohibited.

All Rights Reserved.

The characters and events portrayed in this book are fictitious. Any similarity to real persons, living or dead, is purely coincidental and not intended by the author.

ARE YOU SIGNED UP FOR DRAGONBLADE'S BLOG?

You'll get the latest news and information on exclusive giveaways, exclusive excerpts, coming releases, sales, free books, cover reveals and more.

Check out our complete list of authors, too!

No spam, no junk. That's a promise!

Sign Up Here

www.dragonbladepublishing.com

Dearest Reader;

Thank you for your support of a small press. At Dragonblade Publishing, we strive to bring you the highest quality Historical Romance from some of the best authors in the business. Without your support, there is no 'us', so we sincerely hope you adore these stories and find some new favorite authors along the way.

Happy Reading!

CEO, Dragonblade Publishing

Additional Dragonblade books by Author Aviva Orr

Love and Literature Series
Love and Literature (Book 1)
Love and Vengeance (Book 2)
Love and Liberty (Book 3)

The Lyon's Den Series
The Lyon and The Rose of Mayfair
The Imperfect Lyon

Other Lyon's Den Books

Into the Lyon's Den by Jade Lee
The Scandalous Lyon by Maggi Andersen
Fed to the Lyon by Mary Lancaster
The Lyon's Lady Love by Alexa Aston
The Lyon's Laird by Hildie McQueen
The Lyon Sleeps Tonight by Elizabeth Ellen Carter
A Lyon in Her Bed by Amanda Mariel
Fall of the Lyon by Chasity Bowlin
Lyon's Prey by Anna St. Claire
Loved by the Lyon by Collette Cameron
The Lyon's Den in Winter by Whitney Blake
Kiss of the Lyon by Meara Platt
Always the Lyon Tamer by Emily E K Murdoch
To Tame the Lyon by Sky Purington
How to Steal a Lyon's Fortune by Alanna Lucas
The Lyon's Surprise by Meara Platt
A Lyon's Pride by Emily Royal
Lyon Eyes by Lynne Connolly
Tamed by the Lyon by Chasity Bowlin
Lyon Hearted by Jade Lee
The Devilish Lyon by Charlotte Wren
Lyon in the Rough by Meara Platt
Lady Luck and the Lyon by Chasity Bowlin
Rescued by the Lyon by C.H. Admirand
Pretty Little Lyon by Katherine Bone
The Courage of a Lyon by Linda Rae Sande
Pride of Lyons by Jenna Jaxon
The Lyon's Share by Cerise DeLand
The Heart of a Lyon by Anna St. Claire
Into the Lyon of Fire by Abigail Bridges
Lyon of the Highlands by Emily Royal

The Lyon's Puzzle by Sandra Sookoo
Lyon at the Altar by Lily Harlem
Captivated by the Lyon by C.H. Admirand
The Lyon's Secret by Laura Trentham
The Talons of a Lyon by Jude Knight
The Lyon and the Lamb by Elizabeth Keysian
To Claim a Lyon's Heart by Sherry Ewing
A Lyon of Her Own by Anna St. Claire
Don't Wake a Sleeping Lyon by Sara Adrien
The Lyon and the Bluestocking by E.L. Johnson
The Lyon's Perfect Mate by Cerise DeLand
The Lyon Who Loved Me by Tracy Sumner
Lyon of the Ton by Emily Royal
The Lyon's Redemption by Sandra Sookoo
Truth or Lyon by Katherine Bone
Luck of the Lyon by Belle Ami
The Lyon, the Liar and the Scandalous Wardrobe by Chasity Bowlin
Lyon's Roar by Tabetha Waite
The Lyon's First Choice by Sara Adrien
The Lady of a Lyon by Linda Rae Sande
The Lyon's Paw by Jenna Jaxon
Hook, Lyon and Sinker by Jude Knight
A Lyon to Die For by E.L. Johnson
The Lyon's Gambit by Ruth A. Casie
My Own Private Lyon by Katherine Bone
Saved by the Lyon by Laura Landon
The Lyon and The Rose of Mayfair by Aviva Orr
The Lyon and His Promise by Sherry Ewing
In Service to a Lyon by E.L. Johnson
The Lyon's Golden Touch by Sara Adrien
The Lyon's Saving Grace by C.H. Admirand
Only a Lyon Will Do by Sherry Ewing
Dreaming of a Lyon by Sandra Sookoo
Thrown to the Lyon by Jude Knight
The Lyon's Alliance by Ruth A. Casie

CHAPTER ONE

Mayfair, London, 1815

OLIVER HARRINGTON, 4TH Earl of Knox, sipped his brandy and contemplated the finely crafted dining room table before him, the length of which seemed to stretch on forever. Sixteen high-backed, buttoned leather chairs stood at attention around the mahogany masterpiece, waiting in vain to be filled. It struck Oliver as absurd. Such a stately piece, laden with ostentatious dishes and attended by two footmen, all for one man. *Preposterous.*

He would laugh if he were still capable of doing so. But fate had been a cruel master and had stolen all his joy. First, it had robbed him of his ability to sire children, then it had snatched the love of his life from his arms, and today, he'd received word that it had eliminated his heir.

He hadn't known the young man in question—a distant cousin he'd put off locating for years when he'd still clung to the hope of one day siring his own son and heir. But when his darling had died after a sudden and unexpected illness, that dream had ended. At the time, he'd barely been able to muster the strength to get out of bed, let alone locate the man who would take what should have belonged to the son he'd never have. That was two years ago—two years of his lawyers pressing him to act—even though he was only five and thirty and hardly at death's door. But solicitors were persistent buggers, and they'd become relentless after he swore never to remarry, so he'd finally acquiesced and permitted the search to start. It had taken longer than expected to locate the man next in line to inherit his title and estate—apparently, the young man was somewhat of a roamer and had been on the continent for quite some time. But they'd finally managed to pin him down and deliver the good news. Only a few days later, tragedy struck.

> My Lord,
>
> It is with great regret that we inform you that shortly after locating your sixth cousin and heir, Mathew James Harrington, we received news that the gentleman is deceased. Mr. Harrington was involved in a fatal carriage collision in Nottingham earlier this week. The local magistrate has confirmed the identity of the deceased. As such, we will continue our search for whomever is next in line to inherit your title and estate.
>
> Yours sincerely,
> Huxley and Bailey
> Solicitors at Law

Oliver sighed. The poor gentleman had only just discovered that he would one day inherit the esteemed title of earl. He'd hardly had the time to savor the news before his life had prematurely ended. Alas, it seemed that any unlucky soul attached to Oliver met with an early demise. Perhaps, he should put off searching for the next in line until after his death. Let the poor sod—whomever he was—live in peace. The lawyers could locate the chap when Oliver was gone and no longer posed a threat—and since he was still a relatively young man himself, that could be years away. This was not a problem that needed to be dealt with now. It was time to call off the legal dogs.

Oliver glanced at his plate. The succulent beef, delicate potatoes, and sauteed vegetables had grown cold. But that did not matter. He had little appetite. He closed his eyes and imagined an earlier, happier time. He saw his beautiful Beatrice sitting beside him as she used to—her brunette curls coiled atop her head, her dark, soulful eyes gazing into his, and her dazzling smile brightening the room. Guests filled the seats at their table, chatting and laughing as they ate, drank, and suffused his and Beatrice's home with merriment. How happy they'd been. How wonderful life had been then.

At first, the ton had frowned upon Oliver's choice of bride. Beatrice had been the widow of a successful merchant, and he, an earl, had been expected to marry within the peerage. Despite expectations, Oliver had followed his heart and married for love. And he'd made the right choice. Beatrice had won over the ton, spreading light and laughter wherever she went, despite what she had suffered.

Beatrice had not only lost a husband, but she'd also lost the babe she'd once cherished, and Oliver had wanted nothing more than to give her a new family. But a babe never came to them. Beatrice had not been to blame. She'd conceived and given birth to a healthy babe once before. The problem had lain with him. Perhaps, he'd been thrown from his horse too many times as a boy, or mayhap he'd injured himself climbing a tree. Possibly, there was no rational explanation. Perhaps, he'd simply been born impaired.

Month after month, for years on end, he'd witnessed his wife's disappointment and suffering each time blood stained her sheets. But she'd been an eternal optimist and remained convinced they would one day conceive. After all, her husband was as virile as any healthy young man. There was a time that even Oliver believed, but as the years passed, and Beatrice's womb remained empty, he lost all hope, and his failure weighed heavily on his shoulders. He'd wanted to be the perfect husband, but how could he have achieved that when he was an imperfect man?

It was selfish of me to marry you. I am flawed.

You are perfection. You are all I desire. All I need. You are enough, she'd say, and make love to him with a fervor that reassured him and solidified their bond. Nothing else had mattered. They'd had each other. They'd had all they needed to be happy.

He opened his eyes to the stark emptiness and cold silence of the room, and a searing pain filled his chest.

Don't mourn me forever. Promise me, you'll be happy. Those were her last words to him as she lay on her deathbed. And he'd not even been able to fulfill his final promise to her.

The ache in his chest spread like a burning flame, scorching his throat, face, ears, and eyes.

"Enough!" He slammed his fist onto the table and stood up.

"My lord?" An alarmed footman rushed forward.

"I can't take it anymore," Oliver said, more to himself than the footman.

"I'm sorry. What do you mean, my lord?"

"The silence. I can't take the silence."

"Shall I arrange for music while you dine, my lord?"

"No!" Oliver barked. "Order my horse and carriage to be readied. I'm going out."

"Yes, my lord." The footman bowed and hurried out of the dining room.

Ten minutes later, Oliver strode out his front door toward his awaiting carriage.

"Where to, my lordship?" The driver asked.

"Cleveland Street," Oliver said as he climbed inside his black landau, "The Lyon's Den."

*Two Weeks Later
Yorkshire, England*

"WE WERE GOING to be married." Kate Sheldon spoke in a deathly whisper as she crouched in the corner of her pink cushioned window seat and stared out at the lashing rain.

"Married?" Her aunt, tall and slender like Kate, sank onto the bench beside her niece. "He promised you marriage?"

Kate nodded. "None of this would have mattered if he'd lived," she said, turning to her aunt. "He was going to speak to Papa as soon as he returned from his trip to London." Fresh tears slid from her sore, puffy eyes. "How could I have known fate would be so cruel?"

"I can hardly believe this." Aunt Jane swallowed. "I had no idea—"

"No one knew. Except for Emilia. It was our secret."

"Emilia." Her aunt shook her head "Such a sweet, polite young lady, and all this time, her brother was courting you in secret while your father and I remained ignorant. I should have paid you more attention, but I could never have guessed—never have dreamed you would give yourself away—Oh, Kate!"

"Theo loved me! And Emilia was a dear, loyal friend—my only friend. She wanted me to be her sister. She was so happy that we were going to be family." Kate watched a tree branch whip violently back and forth. "Now they are both dead. My dearest friend and my only love."

Aunt Jane reached for Kate's hand. "Oh, my darling. It may very well be the shock and stress that has caused this delay in your bleeding. You've been so distraught since receiving news of the accident. You've hardly eaten a bite or slept a wink."

"It's not the shock." Kate wiped a tear from her cheek. "I've known for weeks."

"How many weeks, exactly?" Aunt Jane asked in a halting voice as if she were afraid of the answer.

"It's a little over six now, but it was only four when I told Theo—just before the accident. I knew right away when I missed my monthly courses. It had never happened before. That's when Theo proposed. He said all would be well. He had a way to make Papa let me go."

"You might be wrong. It's still very early. There's still a possibility that—"

"I have been sick every day this past week. I swore my maid to secrecy because I didn't want you or Papa to call for the doctor, but I cannot hide the truth from you any longer."

Aunt Jane put a hand over her mouth as if to stave off her words, but her pained expression spoke volumes. *How could you have been so foolish!*

"I *was* foolish," Kate admitted out loud. "But, put yourself in my shoes. I'm five and twenty and destined to be my father's companion for the rest of my life. With two wives in the grave and three younger daughters available to make good marriages, Papa has planned for me to be his keeper in his dotage. That is why he never allowed me to debut into society." Kate smiled to herself. "Theo made me feel like a woman. I couldn't believe my luck. Finally, I'd met a man—a beautiful, caring man—who wanted to marry me. I'd found my own happiness, despite Papa's determination to keep me for himself."

"I feel terrible," her aunt said. "I didn't realize you felt so alone. I should have done more for you—my sister's only child. I've been selfish. I should have come to Yorkshire years ago and insisted your papa let you come out into society. I wrote him about it, and I meant to visit in person, but time just slipped away. And now that I am finally here, it is too late."

"It was one excuse after another, starting with the death of my stepmother. Year after year, Papa kept finding excuses until I was too old to debut. But it's not your fault. You had your own grievances to cope with—"

Aunt Jane pressed her lips together as if to suppress her inner pain, and Kate felt instantly guilty. Her aunt had lost three babes during her marriage—before her husband tragically passed on—and it had caused her years of anguish.

"I'm sorry," Kate said. "I shouldn't have mentioned—"

Aunt Jane straightened her shoulders and inhaled deeply. "That is all in the past. There is nothing we can do to change what has already occurred. What we need to do now is solve the problem at hand."

"There is only one thing to be done," Kate said. "I must leave the country before the truth comes to light or risk my sisters' futures."

"Leave the country?" Aunt Jane raised her eyebrows. "And where do you think you will go? A woman in your condition alone?"

Kate shook her head. "I don't know. Perhaps to the continent."

"Yes, that is one option." Aunt Jane twisted the wedding ring on her finger. "There are families desperate for children who will gladly take you in until you birth the child."

Kate jerked her head up. "That's not what I'm saying. I won't give my babe away. I can pose as a widow and find work."

"Oh, my darling, Kate." Aunt Jane brushed a long chestnut strand from Kate's face. "How naive you are. How protected you have been from this cruel world. What you say is impossible. Both you and your babe would starve to death if you went out in this fierce world alone. And I, for one, will never let that happen."

"Then what can be done? If I stay, we will all be ruined. If it were only my reputation at stake, then I could remain and face the consequences of my actions, but my sisters are innocent. Why should they be punished for my mistake? If the truth comes to light, they will never make a good match. Our family's reputation will be irreparably tarnished."

"I know." Aunt Jane turned to the mullioned window and tightened the shawl around her shoulders as she gazed at the storm raging outside. The rain had joined forces with the wind, making it more powerful. Together they assailed the windowpane, shaking and rattling it with the anger of a jealous god.

Kate flinched. Her aunt was right. The world, which had seemed so bright and full of hope a few weeks earlier, now seemed cold and frightening. But how could she give up her innocent babe to strangers? How could she dishonor Theo's memory by abandoning his child? She could not—would not. She'd die first.

"We must find you a husband before it's too late," Aunt Jane's voice cut into Kate's thoughts.

She turned slowly from the windowpane to face her aunt, wondering if she'd imagined the words. "Whatever do you mean by that? Who would marry me in my condition?"

"It's early yet, and you will likely not show for the next month or two. If we find you a suitable match and you marry within that time frame, he will believe the babe is his." Kate blinked. Her aunt sat upright, her back straight and her face determined. It was as though she'd transformed into an entirely different being.

"You will tell Papa to arrange a marriage for me under false pretenses?" Kate could hardly believe such a thing was possible. "He will never agree."

"Not your papa." Aunt Jane formed a steeple with her hands as she often did when deep in thought. "There's only one person capable of arranging such a marriage."

"Who?" Kate stared at her aunt.

"The Black Widow of Whitehall." Aunt Jane rose from her seat.

"The what?" Kate gazed in bewilderment at her aunt, wondering if she'd gone mad.

"Instruct your maid to ready your bags. We leave for London tomorrow morning."

"But what will you tell Papa?" Kate stood.

"Oh, do stop worrying about your papa so much. He is a selfish man and tired of your tears, so he won't object to my taking you to London for a few weeks as long as I promise it will cure you of your melancholy. And before he has a chance to complain that we've been gone too long, you'll be married and free of him forever."

Kate creased her forehead. "But I don't understand—"

"Bags, Kate," her aunt said firmly. "And remember, you are not to mention anything about the Black Widow of Whitehall to your papa."

Kate nodded in bewilderment as her aunt, seemingly energized by her bizarre plan, hurried out of the room.

Who on Earth is the Black Widow of Whitehall? The name sounded rather frightening and sent shivers down Kate's spine. *Still, if Aunt Jane believes so strongly in this widow, then she must be a miracle maker. At least, she'd better be one because only a miracle can help me now.*

Chapter Two

One week later
Cleveland Street, London

Bessie Dove-Lyon contemplated the young woman sitting before her. She had a coltish look about her—tall and slender with large dark eyes sheltered beneath thick, long lashes, an upturned nose, and a mane of lush chestnut curls. Under normal circumstances, finding her a husband would be challenging—she was five-and-twenty with only a modest dowry—but given her current predicament, it might be near impossible. Well, nothing was impossible—not for Bessie Dove-Lyon, the Black Widow of Whitehall.

She'd arranged hundreds of successful marriages and would no doubt arrange hundreds more. But, with this one, she'd have to tread carefully. Deceiving a man into marrying a woman already with child was a tricky business. Most of Harley Street frequented her establishment, and there were doctors who could be relied upon for their silence. Still, she preferred not to go that route. A better solution was to find a man who would accept a woman already with child. Such a delicate situation required the right kind of man. Ideally, someone who loved without conditions. Someone who'd be a devoted family man, no matter the circumstances. Someone who had loved and lost, who lived with the pain and silence, and who thought he could never find happiness again. Someone like...the answer provided itself in a flash: Lord Oliver Knox.

She'd been observing the Earl of Knox closely for over a month. He came into the club every night, rain or shine. And Bessie suspected that he did so to stave off his loneliness. He had been a devoted husband to his late wife—that was common knowledge—and he'd been devastated by her sudden death, shutting himself away for two years before he started frequenting the Lyon's Den.

He enjoyed the card games and fine brandy but never indulged in the women upstairs. So she suspected his devotion and loyalty to his dead wife remained as strong as it had been during her lifetime. He came to her establishment to ease the painful silence that had become his world. Yes, she'd come across men like him before. And she knew the cure. He needed a new wife—and not just any wife—someone compassionate and loyal as she suspected Kate was, after hearing her story and spending some time in conversation with her. She was the type who could fill his heart and home with joy again—and what could bring a lonely earl more joy than a son and heir?

"I realize the situation is problematic," the young lady's aunt, Mrs. Jane Seton, said, "but time is of the essence. If something cannot be arranged within a few weeks, I'm afraid it will be too late."

"Indeed," Bessie mused. "You have presented me with a most challenging task. Fortunately for you, I enjoy a well-paid challenge."

"That will not be a problem." Mrs. Seton opened her reticule and extracted two banknotes. "My late husband left me a generous sum when he died, and I have no children of my own, so I can see no better use for this money than securing a future for my departed sister's only child."

"Oh, Aunt!" Kate exclaimed. "I couldn't let you—"

"Hush!" Mrs. Seaton rested a hand on Kate's arm. "I'm doing this for my sister and for the good of the family—it will save your sisters much heartache and preserve their reputations. But most of all, I am doing this for you and your babe. I know what it is to lose a child, and I won't let that happen to you."

"And it so happens," Bessie interrupted, wanting to return to the business at hand, "that I have a suitable candidate in mind."

"So soon?" Kate gave a little jump, reminding Bessie of a skittish pony.

"Who is he?" Mrs. Seaton stood up and placed the banknotes on Bessie's desk.

Bessie smiled under her veil as she reached for the banknotes and secured them in her desk drawer. Then she picked up a silver bell and gave it a quick shake.

Almost immediately, her wolf Hermia appeared.

"Locate Lord Knox and ask him to join me in my office."

"Certainly," Hermia said before disappearing again.

"Am I to meet with the gentleman right away?" Kate half rose out of her seat as though she wished to escape. "I'm not prepared."

"No, you are to go downstairs with your aunt and mingle, while I have a private word with the earl."

"An earl!" Mrs. Seaton and Kate exclaimed together.

"I'm amazed," Mrs. Seaton said. "I knew we were right to come to you, but I never imagined—an earl—you say?"

"Don't get too excited. There's no guarantee he will accept my proposal, but I am known to be quite persuasive."

"No!" Kate's eyes grew wider than they already were. "I couldn't possibly—not an earl—not in my condition!"

"Let me worry about those details. That's what your aunt paid me for." Bessie removed the small gold key from her neck and locked her desk drawer. "As I said, there's no guarantee that the earl will be interested in my proposition, but if not him then we'll find another solution. I'm a woman of my word. Your aunt paid dearly for a service, and I shall deliver." She put a gentle hand on Kate's back as she escorted the two women to the door, "Now, the earl is on his way up, so you'd best get downstairs and familiarize yourself with my wonderful establishment."

Mrs. Seaton thanked Bessie once again before the widow closed her office door and smiled to herself. If Hermia had managed to locate the earl in a timely manner, Bessie's two potential lovers would pass each other in the passageway as he made his way upstairs and she made her way downstairs. *That will set the stage for what's to unfold*, she thought with satisfaction. *A glimpse of potential love is a glimpse into a future ripe with hope and that is what dreams are made of. What could be more enticing or powerful?*

THE STATUESQUE, BROAD-SHOULDERED Hermia looked more like a Greek Amazonian warrior than a hostess at a gaming club, Oliver thought as he followed her up the red-carpeted staircase. She was taking him to see Mrs. Dove-Lyon, who'd asked for a word in private with him.

Oliver wasn't surprised. All the men who frequented the Lyon's Den knew that the Black Widow arranged marriages on the side. A woman in some sort of trouble or even just trying to avoid spinsterhood would pay a hefty sum to marry an earl like himself and restore her reputation in society. But he'd have to disappoint Mrs. Dove-Lyon because he had no intention of ever remarrying. Nonetheless, he'd listen to what she had to say out of politeness before letting her know where he stood on the matter.

He followed Hermia down a long corridor illuminated by multiple candelabras affixed to the walls. Two women walking in the opposite direction passed them, greeting Hermia with light nods. There was nothing unusual about this, as both women and men moved freely throughout the Lyon's Den. There was even a women's gaming hall located on the second floor. The Lyon's Den was a kingdom unto its own, with its own rules quite different from those in the outside world—set by its very own queen—Bessie Dove-Lyon.

As the women passed, the younger of the two—or more specifically her eyes, large, dark, and doleful—caught Oliver's attention. Those eyes, soulful like his wife's, told a story of love and loss—a story Oliver knew only too well. The momentary connection was fleeting as they passed each other, but it seemed to stop time and buried itself in Oliver's heart.

He mused on this as the wolf led him to the widow's office and opened the door for him after a knock and a murmured "enter" from within. He stepped into the room. "Lord Knox," Mrs. Dove-Lyon, dressed in her signature black veiled ensemble, stood to greet him. "Thank you for coming. May I offer you a drink?" she asked.

"Brandy, thank you," he said.

She poured his drink and invited him to sit on a plush scarlet armchair, seating herself across from him on a matching sofa. A table laden with a silver tea tray stood between them, and she leaned forward to fill her cup. "I am always happy to meet new patrons. How are you enjoying the Lyon's Den?"

"Very much," he said.

She leaned back onto the sofa, leaving her tea untouched. "I am pleased. You have been here every night for over a month now."

"Is that a problem?" he asked.

"Not at all. But I'm curious to know what draws you here. I've been in business for many years, and you've never been a patron before."

He nodded and sipped his brandy, not wanting to dredge up the old pain but not seeing a way out of this conversation. "I was a happily married man for eight years, but my wife died quite unexpectedly two years ago, and I—" his throat seemed to close on his words.

"You come here to assuage the loneliness," the widow said.

He stared into his glass, then lifted it to his mouth and drained the golden liquid. It slid down his throat and warmed his chest. "Something like that," he said, turning his eyes back onto her. He didn't need to say more. He supposed she understood since she'd lost her husband, though he knew nothing of her past or her married life. Not everyone's marriage was as blissful as his had been.

"But you could do that at any gaming establishment. What I want to know is why you have chosen mine?"

He shrugged. "It's no secret that you serve the finest wine and brandy," he saluted her with his glass, "as well as many other discrete services."

"That's right." She nodded and then paused as if she were waiting for him to say more. When he remained silent, she said, "But you are not a man who cares for those discrete services, are you?"

Sorrow engulfed Oliver, rendering him unable to respond. He hadn't been able to bear the thought of another woman after his Beatrice died.

"Lord Knox, it is no secret that I arrange marriages, so I was wondering if you chose to frequent my establishment in the hopes of finding a new bride?"

Here it is. Thank heavens. Now, I can put an end to this conversation. "I'm aware of the services you provide, but I'm afraid I am not here for that reason. I have no intention of remarrying."

She cocked her head. "Were you and your wife blessed with children, Lord Knox?"

He shifted in his seat. The widow's questions were starting to stab at his heart like knife wounds. He didn't want to be having this conversation. "No," he said abruptly.

"Then your wife was barren?"

This time the knife plunged deeper into his chest. "My wife was a perfectly healthy woman—a perfect woman in every way," he said, his throat tight.

"But eight years and no heir? Clearly, she was—"

He held up his hand to stave off her words. He could not tolerate his wife's memory being defiled so. Beatrice had not been at fault. It was him—he was flawed. He could not let this stand!

"The fault didn't lie with my wife," he blurted.

The widow remained silent behind her veil, no doubt.

He sighed. "She'd been married once before. During that union, she conceived and birthed a healthy daughter. But both her husband and child perished when their carriage overturned. A year later, she married me, and in our eight years together I failed to give her a child."

"You can't be certain about that. Your wife could have developed a problem that wasn't present in her younger years. The fault could still have been hers."

"It wasn't her fault!" he said. His heart clenched like a fist as the memories of Beatrice's tears assailed him. "For eight years, I felt my wife's pain as she waited in vain to hold her own babe in her arms. I won't do it again."

The widow nodded.

He had a strong urge to leave the room. Why was he here discussing his most painful and private life with this woman? How dare she speak to him about such matters? He ought to leave this club and never return.

"I apologize if this conversation upset you, Lord Knox. That was not my intention. I do have good reason for my inquiry, and the situation is quite delicate." She leaned forward. "Are you willing to hear my proposal?"

Oliver's anger softened in response to the widow's apology. She obviously had good intentions, no doubt believing she could pair him with some young woman and bring him happiness again. He eyed her black attire and wondered why she chose to dress thus when she'd been a widow for several years. Did she still mourn her husband? Why hadn't she taken her own advice and remarried? People said she was married to her work, and that seemed to be the truth. She was a formidable woman who ruled her club with an iron fist. Still, she understood loss—that much was obvious. Mayhap, it would behoove him to listen to what she had to say.

"Go on." He nodded.

"A young woman was just in my office. She came to see me because she has an urgent problem that needs solving."

Doleful eyes. Oliver straightened, suddenly eager to hear more.

"You see, she was betrothed to a young man. It was a love match." Mrs. Dove-Lyon cleared her throat. "Unfortunately, the young man died unexpectedly, leaving his betrothed in a rather delicate situation that requires her to find a husband immediately."

"Do you mean that she's with child?" Oliver said.

Mrs. Dove-Lyon nodded. "There are no outward signs yet. No one would know the child wasn't yours."

Oliver put down his brandy glass. "What are you saying? Are you suggesting that I"—he shook his head—"I already told you that I have no intention of remarrying." He stood, intent on leaving.

"If what you have told me is true, this could be your only chance to have a family—and an heir."

Oliver stiffened. "Are you suggesting that I pass on my title and estate to a child who's not my own?" He bristled at the notion—not because of some archaic law, but because he could not endure the thought of raising a child with another woman. "As opposed to some distant cousin you know nothing about?" Mrs. Dove-Lyon stood, retrieved Oliver's empty glass from the table, and went to pour him another brandy. Clearly, no matter what he thought, the conversation wasn't over. Especially when she turned to him and said, "A child you raise from birth and love as your own—a child who calls you 'papa'—becomes your child. Blood is not what makes a parent."

He wasn't able to dispute her logic. Instead, he accepted the brandy she handed him and peered into its amber depths.

Then he returned to his plush armchair. "It wouldn't be right," he said, finally taking a sip of the brandy. "My title will pass to the next in line. Whomever that may be."

"Lord Knox, if I had done what others deemed to be right and proper, I'd be in the poor house as we speak. We must all take responsibility for our own happiness. And this is your chance to fill your home with love and laughter again."

"I wish that were true. But you do not have an earl's responsibilities," he said because it was easier to hide behind his earldom than to tell the truth. He would have raised a foundling with Beatrice if she'd so desired. But his hope becoming a father had died with her. He put down his glass and stood up. "I'm sorry, but I cannot," he said, nodding to her before he left the room.

Bessie was not convinced. Lord Knox was a family man at heart, but he was afraid. He didn't ever want to relive the hurt he'd experienced after losing his wife. He hated the loneliness, but he wasn't willing to risk any more pain. Such problems weren't insurmountable. A man like Lord Knox could be won over. Unfortunately, Miss Sheldon didn't have that kind of time. She needed a husband and father for her baby, and she needed one now. It appeared as though Bessie would have to take more drastic measures.

CHAPTER THREE

KATE'S INSIDES CHURNED as she accepted a cup of tea from Mrs. Dove-Lyon. She hadn't expected to return to the widow's office so soon. The woman worked quickly. Hadn't she only met with the earl yesterday evening? She glanced at her aunt, who clutched her teacup handle, looking equally anxious.

The wife of an earl. Can it be true? Even Papa will not refuse such a prestigious match!

"I'm afraid the gentleman I had in mind for you is unwilling." Mrs. Dove-Lyon's words slashed Kate's expectations, making her stomach plummet. "Unfortunately, he had too many reservations. Under normal circumstances, we wouldn't give up so easily, and although I think he is amenable to changing his mind, we simply don't have the time to try and sway him."

"What can be done now?" Aunt Jane spoke the question Kate wanted to ask but could not articulate. It seemed fear and shock had captured her voice. She'd been foolish to assume the news would be good. *Why on Earth would an earl want to marry me?*

"Considering the time constraint, I propose an auction. It's not something I do often, but it's worked well in the past."

Kate flinched.

"An auction?" Aunt Jane exclaimed. "That's going too far. I cannot permit my niece to be sold like cattle. What kind of a man would purchase a wife?"

"It's a blind auction," Mrs. Dove-Lyon explained calmly, as though she'd expected exactly such a reaction from Kate's protective aunt. "The men won't know who or what they are bidding on. I will merely announce that the prize is a lifelong treasure—something priceless—something every man will covet. Furthermore, all the men will be given numbers and be required to wear masks so no one will know the winner's identity. Your identity and his identity will be kept from everyone."

Aunt Jane put down her teacup with shaking hands. "It's too repulsive. I cannot allow it. And what if a married man bids on her?"

"You needn't worry about that. I shall only invite my unmarried clients to participate in the auction," Mrs. Dove-Lyon said.

"Well, then, they will certainly have an inkling that they are bidding on a woman. Again, I shall have to ask what kind of a gentleman would participate in such an event?"

"A very drunk one. There is a reason I serve my customers the finest wine, brandy, and whiskey in all of England. They are gluttons for it, and that gets them into all sorts of troubling situations."

"You plan to marry my Kate to a drunkard?" Aunt Jane reached for Kate and put a protective hand on her forearm.

"Of course not. The auction is a game with high stakes and men like to drink when they play. But habitual drunkards will not be invited to participate. Those men are trouble and are carefully monitored at my club."

Kate sat frozen, staring into her teacup. She'd been such a fool—a fool to lay with Theo before they were married—a fool to imagine she could marry an earl—a fool to think any man worth his salt would marry her—a fool to hope she might ever be happy again.

"It sounds too ridiculous," Aunt Jane said. "I don't believe it can work."

"Mrs. Seton, I don't waste my time on schemes that won't work." There was a sharp edge to Mrs. Dove-Lyon's voice. "I know my patrons, and I know men. They are competitive creatures. I will plant two or three gentlemen who owe me favors in with the crowd, and they will get the bidding started. Then, you will see the bullish nature of wealthy, drunk men emerging in full force. I guarantee you will have barons, viscounts, and earls waging a bidding war for your niece's hand in marriage."

"Even so, I can't—no, I can't allow this."

"Why don't we let Miss Sheldon decide." The widow turned to Kate. "It is time for her to speak up and take control of her future."

Momentarily panicked, Kate glanced at her aunt. She didn't want to go against her wishes.

"Don't look to your aunt," the widow snapped. "We know her opinion. And before you say anything, I'd like to remind you of your pressing circumstance."

"Is there truly no other way?" Kate placed a protective hand on her belly.

"Considering the pressing issue of the growing babe in your womb—your options are limited. You have gotten yourself into a serious predicament, and that puts me in a bind as well. I need to protect my interests and reputation as well as yours. I must proceed with caution so as not to arrange a marriage for you that might later become a problem for me."

"What do you mean?" Kate asked. "What risk is there to you?"

Mrs. Dove-Lyon sighed. "If by some chance the gentleman you marry discovers that the child you are carrying is not his, I don't want him coming back to me, complaining that I deliberately tricked him into marrying a woman with child. If, however, a man 'wins' your hand in a blind auction—an auction he willingly bid on—then he will only have his drunken foolishness to blame and so will shoulder the responsibility for the match."

The color drained from Kate's face. "Do you think he will discover the child is not his?"

"Anything is possible. But I think the chances are slim. You are very slight, and your figure shows no signs. Men are quite ignorant when it comes to birthing. Babes often arrive early."

"But the doctor will know—surely."

"Fortunately, many Harley Street doctors are patrons of the Lyon's Den. I will ensure your doctor understands what he is supposed to do for you, your suitor, and my reputation."

Kate swallowed the fear that rose in her throat. She had to do what was best for her child, even if that meant enduring something as humiliating as an auction.

"Your aunt paid me a great deal of money to help you, Miss Sheldon. If you do not allow me to fulfill my task, your aunt will forfeit her contribution. I do not return fees paid. You are free to walk away and solve this problem however you see fit, but the money will be lost to you."

"I don't care about the money, Kate." Aunt Jane reached for Kate's hand. "You don't have to do this. We'll find another solution."

"No," Kate insisted. "You said that Mrs. Dove-Lyon was the best person to come to for help—the only person capable of solving my problem. I trust your judgment, Aunt Jane."

Aunt Jane closed her eyes and sighed. Then she pressed her lips together and nodded her consent.

"I'll do it." Kate turned to the widow.

"Very well," the widow said. "The auction will take place tomorrow evening, but you needn't worry yourself with the details. My staff will take care of everything." Mrs. Dove Lyon picked up her teacup and raised it in Kate's direction. "Just think on it, Miss Sheldon, tomorrow night all of your problems will be over."

Kate raised her teacup, hope and fear warring within her for what the future might hold.

CLOAKED GENTLEMEN, EACH wearing a distinctive animal mask, gathered in the center of the candlelit, smoke-filled room, waving fistfuls of money in the air whilst chanting, "Auction, auction, auction!"

Servants weaved between the gentlemen, carrying silver trays of brandy and whiskey-filled glasses that were quickly emptied and refilled. Having sampled a few glasses himself, Oliver knew the spirits were potent and of the finest quality. The men were indulging, and most of them were heavily intoxicated.

Helena, another of Mrs. Dove-Lyon's female wolves, stood on an elevated podium addressing the gentlemen. She wore a silk red empire dress embellished with peacock feathers and a glittery red mask over her eyes that added to the carnival-like atmosphere in the room. The scene fascinated Oliver, who'd been intrigued when he'd received an exclusive invitation to a blind auction. He had no intention of bidding, but curiosity had compelled him to attend.

"The lucky gentleman who casts the winning bid," Helena announced, silencing the crowd with her surprisingly stentorian voice, "will earn a prize so precious and priceless he will be the envy of all."

The men cheered, clapped, and whistled.

"Who is brave enough to cast the first bid?" Helena scanned the room. "You, sir!" She pointed to a gentleman in a cat mask.

"Twenty pounds," he shouted.

"We've got twenty pounds from the black cat. Are the rest of you fine gentlemen going to let him take the prize for a mere twenty pounds?"

"Twenty-five!" A hand shot up in the middle of the crowd.

"That's twenty-five pounds from the rat. Are the rest of you gentlemen going to let a rat outbid you?"

Jeers and shouts erupted from the crowd.

"Thirty!" Another hand raised in the air.

"The hyena thrashes the rat at thirty pounds. Do we have anyone willing to take on a hyena?" Hermia bated the drunk crowd.

"Fifty," a gentleman in a tiger mask shouted.

"Oh, the tiger is showing his claws, gentleman. He's a true fighter. Is there anyone brave enough to take on a tiger?"

"Sixty." The gentleman next to Oliver raised his hand. He wore the face of a green snake.

"The snake has finally come out of the grass and shows his face! Who is going to win this battle, the snake or the tiger?"

"Seventy!" Tiger Mask shouted, and the crowd cheered.

"Ninety!" The snake's determined voice sounded above the ruckus.

Oliver frowned. *These fools don't even know what they are bidding on.*

"How about you?" Helena pointed at Oliver. "Is the King of Beasts going to join this fight?"

"Lion, Lion, Lion!" the crowd chanted.

Oliver shook his head.

"Lion, Lion, Lion!" the men chanted, but Oliver continued to shake his head.

"One hundred pounds!" Tiger Mask shouted.

The room exploded with cheers. "Tiger, Tiger, Tiger!"

"One hundred and ten!" Oliver's snake-masked neighbor shouted above the ruckus.

Whistles and applause followed his bid. "Snake, Snake, Snake," the crowd chanted.

"One hundred and ten pounds to the snake! Does anyone wish to bid one hundred and fifteen? This is your last chance to be a winner! What do you say, King of Beasts? Is it time to step in and snatch your prey from this weaker opponent?"

"Lion, Lion, Lion!" the men chanted, but Oliver continued to shake his head.

"And you, Tiger? Are you going to let this silly little grass snake tame you?"

"One hundred and twenty," Tiger Mask shouted.

One hundred and forty," Snake Mask bellowed without a moment's hesitation.

"Tiger, Tiger, Tiger!" The crowd chanted, wanting to keep the game going, but the gentleman in the tiger mask shook his head and turned out his pockets.

"Then I declare the gentleman snake our winner!"

Cheers and deafening applause filled the room.

"Gentlemen," Hermia bellowed over the noise, "keep your masks and cloaks in place as you exit through the two back doors. A servant will strip you of your disguises as you pass through the darkened exit room one at a time."

Just then, Puck and Theseus, two of Mrs. Dove-Lyon's male wolves, appeared and started herding the men toward the exits. Oliver stayed where he stood, deciding it was wise to wait for the crowd to dissipate before exiting. "This is utter madness. "Oliver said, turning to his snake-masked neighbor as Helena weaved her way through the crowd toward them. "You just paid one hundred and forty pounds for Lord knows what."

"Oh, I am certain it will be worth my while," Snake Mask said.

"Gentlemen." Helena approached them. "Good evening."

Both Oliver and Snake Mask bowed in response.

"May I escort you to Mrs. Dove-Lyon's office? she said, addressing the snake-masked winner. "She has some papers for you to sign."

"Papers?" Oliver remarked, wondering what sort of prize could involve paperwork.

"Indeed." Snake Mask rubbed his hands together. "And will I be meeting my prize this evening?"

"Of course," Helena said. "As soon as the money has been paid in full."

Oliver frowned as he watched Snake Mask follow Helena out a third exit, which no doubt led to Mrs. Dove-Lyon's office.

Something very odd is afoot, he thought as he turned to leave. *Something very odd, indeed.*

Chapter Four

He was watching her. The earl. She was certain it was him—the one Mrs. Dove Lyon had said was perfect for her. The handsome, sandy-haired gentleman whose smoldering gray eyes had locked on hers as they'd passed each other in the passageway upstairs after her first meeting with Mrs. Dove-Lyon. It had only been a moment, but the memory of their brief connection had made her stomach leap. It was the same sensation she'd felt the first time she'd seen Theo, the memory of whom still brought an ache to her throat and tears to her eyes.

Stop it! She chastised herself, remembering that the earl had had no interest in meeting her and that she was now bound to the man who stood before her. His name was Lord Middlemarch—a mealy-mouthed, pale, baron. His lips were thin, his eyes small and watery, and his smile insincere. Every time they spoke, he made it clear that he thought himself better than her. Her stomach churned as his mouth moved. He liked to talk about himself and his accomplishments—which mostly included what he inherited. Not once had he asked her about herself, her family, her wants, her needs, or her dreams. He had made no effort to woo her, this man. And why would he? There was no need for it. He'd purchased her at auction. He owned her, just like a pet poodle.

Her only saving grace was that no one knew she'd been auctioned into marriage. Her identity as well as Middlemarch's had been kept a secret. It saved her the humiliation of people knowing she'd been purchased but not the humiliation of people thinking she'd actually chosen such an odious man to be her husband. The thought made her want to scream. Still, she had to force herself to see the good in him. He was to be her child's father, and he had the means and the title to provide her child with a proper future. In that respect, the auction had been a success.

Kate looked at Middlemarch and tried to imagine her life as his wife. She saw herself entering a ballroom on his arm and shivered. He would no doubt parade her around like a prized mare and then send her to a corner where she would be expected to remain silent for hours while he socialized. And what kind of father would he make? A harsh one she imagined. Someone who belittled his son, letting him know he was never good enough—never as capable and clever as his father.

Oh Theo, why did you have to leave us to the mercy of this man? Our little family. We would have been so happy together!

"Miss Sheldon," Lord Middlemarch said, "You really must do something about your manners. You cannot be daydreaming while a gentleman—your future husband, for that matter—is talking to you. How am I supposed to take you out in public when you behave like this? It will be downright embarrassing. As a wife, it is your duty to serve me, and that means listening when I talk." His mouth pursed into a sour grape like that of a petulant child.

She could stand no more. She'd sooner starve on the streets than marry a man like Lord Middlemarch. Her aunt had paid Mrs. Dove-Lyon a large sum of money and was doling out almost all of her life's savings for Kate's dowry, so the widow simply had to do better!

"We are not yet married, my lord, and if you don't like the way I behave, you may leave," she said, enjoying the momentary slackening of his mouth before his face tightened again.

"How dare you?" He spat the words. "I paid for you, and I own you. You will show me the respect and gratitude I command as your future husband. Do you understand?"

She straightened her back, ready to give the spineless worm a piece of her mind. "But we are not yet married, and if you—" she began, but was cut off when her aunt suddenly appeared by her side.

"My lord, I'm sorry to interrupt, but I wonder if I may have a word with my niece."

"Take all the time you need, madam. I have decided to retire to the gaming room. If you are able to teach Miss Sheldon how to behave with manners toward her future husband and lord, she may send me a note of apology. Until then, we have nothing further to say to each other. Good evening." He turned and marched toward the gaming room.

"Have you ever encountered such a rude and pompous man!" Kate fumed.

"Outside, please, Katherine." Her aunt clutched her arm and led her across the ballroom through the French patio doors and into the garden. Aunt Jane did not start her lecture until they were safely ensconced in a remote part of the garden. "What in the world has gotten into you?" she asked once they were alone.

"The man is insufferable!" Kate said. "I must speak with Mrs. Dove-Lyon and tell her I cannot marry him. I am sure she will understand and make some other arrangement for me."

"Katherine"—her aunt looked sternly at her—"you entered into a contract where you agreed to participate in that auction, and Mrs. Dove-Lyon doesn't take kindly to those who cost her money and damage her reputation by breaking agreements with her."

"But I can't possibly marry that man." Kate covered her face with her hands.

"Yes, you can"—Aunt Jane lowered her voice—"for the sake of your child, Kate, you must make amends with him. Even if Mrs. Dove-Lyon agreed to let you out of the contract, which I doubt, time is not on your side. Within a few weeks, you will start to show, and what will you do then? Mrs. Dove-Lyon instructed Lord Middleton to get a special license. She said the wedding needed to happen within a few days. That is for your protection. Now, if you want this marriage to take place before your change becomes visible, you must appease Lord Middlemarch."

Kate shook her head, unable to get the words out of her mouth as her throat swelled. "It's not fair," she choked. "I was betrothed to a good man—a man I loved dearly—and because of a terrible accident, I am now forced into an unhappy marriage. What kind of a father will Lord Middlemarch make? He's positively vulgar."

"He'll provide you and your child with security and a title."

"Is that all that matters in the world?"

"Unfortunately, it matters a great deal. Think of your sisters, Kate. Their reputations are at stake."

Kate nodded and wiped away the tear that flowed down her cheek. "I know you are right. I am behaving like a spoiled child. But I do worry if that man is capable of loving and being kind to my child, even if he believes it to be his own. He is so cold."

"He can't be all that bad," her aunt said softly. "You've only just met him, and you've already decided against him. Perhaps, if you try being more gracious to him, he will be more amiable to you."

Kate bit her lip. There was no point in arguing. Her aunt was right. She'd made a terrible mistake—one night of passion had led to this. But she had to think of her sisters and her babe. Her happiness had been stolen from her the day the love of her life and her best friend had been killed in that terrible accident. That day, fate had turned against her. But that didn't give her the right to steal her babe's and her sisters' futures. She couldn't bear to see them suffer. She'd simply have to take comfort in their happiness. They would have a chance to marry for love—but for her, that chance was lost forever.

Guilt plagued Oliver after he'd observed Miss Sheldon's distress. Had Mrs. Dove-Lyon arranged a marriage between her and Lord Middlemarch? If so, Miss Sheldon didn't look too pleased about it. And who could blame her? Judging from Middlemarch's spiteful expression before he'd stalked off, it appeared as though he'd been rather unkind to her.

Oliver stood up and sighed. It was none of his business, yet he felt compelled to investigate. He followed Lord Middlemarch into the gaming room and, upon locating him in a darkened corner, drinking brandy alone at table, sat down beside him.

"Having a good night?" he asked.

"Not entirely." Middlemarch picked up his brandy glass and drained it.

"Who was that lovely young lady I saw you talking to earlier?" Oliver said in a deliberately casual tone.

Middlemarch snorted. "No one special. Just another woman who managed to ensnare a peer into marriage. And she's an ungrateful one too."

Oliver's blood boiled in his veins. But he smiled and pretended to sympathize. "Women want nothing more than your title and money."

"Exactly, and that would be fine if they at least showed a bit of gratitude. But that young lady behaves as though I am doing her a favor by marrying her."

"Marrying her?" Oliver's heart sank. "She's your betrothed?"

Middlemarch nodded.

"How did an intelligent gentleman like you become ensnared by such a conniving young lady?" Oliver tried to keep the sarcasm from his voice.

Apparently, he'd succeeded because Middlemarch grinned. "I'm not supposed to talk about it." He smacked his thin lips in a revolting manner. "Secret."

"Very well, then," Oliver shrugged, knowing that feigning disinterest was the best way for Middlemarch to reveal the secret.

"Let's just say, I was a snake in the grass caught in a lioness's trap."

"A snake?" Realization dawning in on him, Oliver straightened his back. "Was it you who won the auction tonight?"

Middlemarch smirked. "That was me. One hundred and forty pounds for an ungrateful bride."

"What? Are you saying that Mrs. Dove-Lyon auctioned that young woman?" Oliver lowered his voice to a whisper.

"That's correct."

"She was the prize?" Oliver shook his head. "This is utter madness. It cannot be true."

"Oh, I can assure you it is absolutely real," Middlemarch said.

"Did you know that you were bidding on a woman?"

"I knew as much as everyone else here knows that when a gentleman participates in any of Mrs. Dove-Lyon's games, he might end up winning a bride."

"Good God!" Oliver said again. "Did the lady in question know she was being auctioned off like a filly?"

"Not only did she know, but she also most likely paid for the privilege."

"What?" Oliver couldn't hide his surprise.

"Surely you know the widow arranges marriages."

"Arranges them, yes. Auctions off women—no."

"There's more than one way to arrange a marriage. And Mrs. Dove-Lyon is very creative. A desperate woman will pay a hefty sum to secure a husband, especially a baron like myself." Middlemarch sniffed in apparent disgust. "I can only imagine what they would pay for an earl."

Oliver could not believe what he was hearing. *What kind of woman permits herself to be auctioned into marriage? How desperate must her circumstances be*—A sudden thought hit him like a punch to the gut. *A woman who has discovered she is with child out of wedlock would be desperate enough to do such a thing. Did Miss Sheldon agree to auction herself off in order to secure a father for her babe, because I refused Dove-Lyon's offer?* If so, he could not let this marriage go through.

"Interesting," Oliver said, trying not to show his revulsion for Middlemarch or his regard for Miss Sheldon. "And when are you intending to marry the young lady in question?"

"When she learns to show me respect."

"Oh dear," Olive said, swallowing his fury. "It sounds as if you regret your impulsiveness."

"No regrets," Middlemarch said. "She's quite attractive. And I have had a difficult time finding a woman suited to my needs."

"Your needs?" Oliver asked, hoping the conversation wasn't about to become even more repulsive.

"Yes. I want someone young, fertile, and pretty to look at. I think it's a blight on a man to have an unattractive filly on his arm. But she must be desperate and destitute, so that I can mold her—teach her to know her place."

Control her, more the like. Oliver clenched his fists under the table. "Still, this one sounds like more trouble than she is worth."

"On the contrary, I think I will enjoy the challenge."

"The challenge?" Oliver asked.

"Of taming the shrew as Shakespeare put it." Middlemarch sipped his brandy. "That filly needs a firm hand."

Oliver inhaled deeply. It was all he could do to stop himself from hitting the man. *How could Mrs. Dove-Lyon pair the lovely Miss Sheldon with this odious creature? What kind of father will he be to her child?* Oliver shook his head. But who was he to question the Black Widow? She only did what Miss Sheldon had paid her to do—secure her a husband and a father for her unborn babe. In all fairness, Mrs. Dove-Lyon had tried to get him to marry Miss Sheldon, and he'd refused. Yet, he could not stand by and let her marry Middlemarch.

What could be done if they were already betrothed? Any contract with Dove-Lyon would have to be honored.

"To be clear, you haven't set a date for the wedding?" Oliver asked, his mind still churning. He'd need time if he wanted to think of a plan that would work.

"Not yet. We only signed the contract tonight, and I want to see her tamed before I get the license, so she knows my demands are serious. If she wants to be Lady Middlemarch, she will show her loyalty and obedience to me first."

Oliver thought of his fiery Beatrice. How he'd loved her bold spirit. The thought of a man like Middlemarch forcing her, or any woman, into submission made his blood boil. Middlemarch didn't deserve Miss Sheldon or her babe.

"That's a shame." Oliver stood up, overwhelmed by his own grief and anger.

"What do you mean?"

"I quite like a spirited woman. And I think it would be a shame to see Miss Sheldon tamed by the likes of you."

Oliver smiled upon seeing Middlemarch's smug expression crumble. "And one more thing, don't boast about the auction. It only makes you sound like a fool who can't attract a bride based on his own merits."

Then he turned and strode out of the gaming room.

KATE SAT ON a garden bench and breathed in the fresh night air. She needed to compose herself. Her aunt was right. She'd have to apologize to Middlemarch. She'd have to be compliant, and she'd have to maintain that for the rest of her life—for her babe's sake. She cleared the sorrow from her throat and stood up, ready to go inside and face her future.

"Miss Sheldon," a man's voice addressed her.

Her heart pulsed. It was him. The earl. He stood before her, tall, broad-shouldered, and impeccably dressed in a white linen shirt and cravat fitted under a midnight blue waistcoat and matching tailcoat, paired with tan trousers and black top boots. His strong jaw, chiseled features, and mesmerizing eyes were the opposite of Middlemarch's small, mealy face. Looking at him made her want to weep with regret. Why had she let herself be auctioned?

"We haven't had the pleasure of meeting, yet. I'm Lord Knox. I know it's improper to come and introduce myself, but Mrs. Dove-Lyon spoke so highly of you, I feel as if I already know you." He gave her a warm smile—one that softened his features and revealed a genuine kindness of heart.

Her breath caught in her throat. Yet she stiffened at the reference to his conversation with Mrs. Dove-Lyon and turned her face in an effort to shield her embarrassment. "Yes, of course," she murmured, barely able to get the words out.

"I hope I haven't upset you," he said.

She couldn't let him see her being weak, even though that's how she felt. "Just what exactly did Mrs. Dove-Lyon tell you about me?" she asked, turning to face him again.

He ran a hand through his thick, sandy hair and seemed to contemplate his words before saying, "She explained your predicament. And why you are in need of a husband."

"I see." Humiliated beyond anything she'd ever experienced, Kate felt herself stiffen even more as she wondered just how much of her predicament the widow had divulged. "And you obviously wanted no part of that, so why are you here now?"

"That's not entirely true," he said, locking his soft gray eyes on her face, and making her skin tingle. "My circumstances are...well, regardless, I wanted to warn you about Middlemarch. I know the man, and he isn't someone you—or any woman—should spend their life with."

"Do you think I don't know that?" Kate said, embarrassed, but also oddly relieved to be talking about her predicament with this stranger. "I don't have a choice."

He cleared his throat. "I understand. I was present at the auction."

Kate's cheeks flamed. "I don't know what you are talking about."

"I'm sorry. I didn't mean to upset you." His voice was gentle and sincere, making Kate want to gravitate toward its warmth. "I only wanted to tell you that there are ways to extract yourself from a contract. All it takes is a lot of money and a bit of power."

"I don't have any money"—she stopped, suddenly suspicious. "Are you offering to purchase me as well?"

"Not you. Your freedom."

Kate scoffed. "And what shall I do then? Clearly, everyone knows I was auctioned off like a donkey. I'm a laughing stock."

"No one else knows. I can assure you that none of the other participants remember a thing. They were all very drunk."

"I suppose it doesn't matter since I am to be married and quite possibly locked away forever."

"I can't allow that." He inched closer to her "I won't let Middlemarch break you—he will crush your spirit."

"And what concern is my spirit of yours? As I said before, it's my understanding that you told Mrs. Dove-Lyon you wanted nothing to do with me." She could hardly believe her bold words, but fear, humiliation, and frustration made her unapologetic. Why was this man taunting her with his chiseled face and kind words? He didn't want her. He'd made that clear.

"I had my reasons for declining Mrs. Dove-Lyon's proposal—deeply personal reasons. But seeing you with Middlemarch—the way he treats you. I can't let that happen. I wish to help you, and I am in a position to do so."

Kate forced a smile. He felt sorry for her, and she didn't care to be his charity project. Although she could not articulate why. She needed help but taking help from him—a man she wanted despite his rejection—seemed too humiliating. "I thank you for your offer and warning, Lord Knox. Perhaps if the circumstances were different," she said brusquely and straightened her back. It was time to face up to her responsibilities. "Good evening, my lord." She turned and strode away to find her aunt.

Chapter Five

Four days later...

Miss Sheldon had not returned to the Lyon's Den since the night of the auction, but that had not prevented Oliver from thinking about her. He assumed that Middlemarch had her holed up somewhere, forcing her to comply with all his demands before he honored his contract and made an honest woman out of her, and the idea plagued him.

For Oliver, the Lyon's Den had lost its luster. It no longer silenced his pain. But it was still far better than his Park Avenue mansion, where the silence had become especially haunting. He could not sleep and eventually gave up trying. Instead, he took to sitting by the fire in his study all night, a glass of brandy in hand. There he sat, watching the flames, and thinking of his wife's wide beautiful smile and her chocolate eyes that used to make him melt. Is this what he wanted for the rest of his life? To have memories only? To live with this loneliness? This silence? Why should he deny himself another chance at happiness? Would it be so bad to raise another man's child?

Of course not. That was not the problem. It was fear that plagued him. Fear of loss. Fear of pain. Anything was better than experiencing such pain again, even silence.

When the first rays of light seeped through the curtains into the study, he stood and went back to his room, retrieved his morning coat, and left the house. He enjoyed having time alone in the park before it was filled with people selling their wares, promenading, and riding. He loved the peacefulness of the early morning amongst the greenery. He could stand and watch the fowl in St. James's canal for hours.

But on this morning, it seemed that someone else had had the same idea as him. As he approached the canal, he saw the figure of a woman leaning on the Chinese bridge that had been built the previous year as part of the Grand Jubilee celebration. He thought it odd that she was alone. Her dress indicated that she was upper class, and so she should at least have had a maid accompanying her. He mounted the bridge and intended to stroll past, not wanting to disturb the lady, but as he got closer, he saw that her shoulders shook. The woman was weeping. He could not walk away and leave a damsel in distress. That was not in his nature.

"Miss," he said gently, "are you in need of any assistance?"

She turned, a handkerchief pressed to her face, and her dark eyes filled with tears.

It was Miss Sheldon. He stepped back in surprise.

"Lord Knox!" Miss Sheldon pulled the handkerchief from her face. "What are you doing here?"

"I was unable to sleep and stepped out for an early morning walk. What about you? Has something happened? Did someone hurt you? Was it Middlemarch?"

"No, it's nothing. I'm perfectly fine." She sniffed and turned from him.

"Where is your aunt?" he asked, looking around despite the park being empty. "You shouldn't be in the park alone, especially at this hour when no one is about."

"That is the best time to be in the park." She pulled her shawl tighter around her shoulders. "Obviously you know that, or you wouldn't be here yourself."

"But I am a man. It's dangerous for a woman to be here unchaperoned."

"I know." Miss Sheldon sighed. "And thank you for your concern. But I just needed some time alone—to think. It's been so—" She pressed the handkerchief to her eyes. "I'm sorry you had to see me like this."

"But if no one has hurt you, then please tell me what the matter is. As I told you the other night, I want to help."

Miss Sheldon shook her head. "You cannot help me. No one can." She turned back to the canal and gazed at the swans gliding along the water. "I made a mistake, but I am not a bad person. I was betrothed and deeply in love. Have you ever lost anyone dear to you, Lord Knox? The pain is quite unbearable."

His heart went out to her. What had this poor woman done wrong besides love someone? "I know." He leaned his forearms on the bridge and stood beside her gazing at the water. "I lost my wife two years ago. She was the light of my life. Since her death, my world has been dark and silent. It's the silence that I find most unbearable. That's why I frequent the Lyon's Den. The noise provides some relief."

"How did she die?" Oliver felt Miss Sheldon's eyes on him.

He turned to her and swallowed. Her eyes were so like Beatrice's that he had to force himself not to look away again as he relived the painful memory. "She developed a headache," he said. "I sent her to lie down with a cup of tea, but she couldn't rest. The pain grew worse. I gave her some laudanum, and it eased her pain enough to allow her to sleep. She awoke in the middle of the night after the drug had worn off in excruciating agony. She knew then that she was dying. She told me so and begged me to be happy after she was gone. I refused to accept it and sent one of my servants to fetch the doctor, but she died before he arrived."

"How horrible," Miss Sheldon said.

"I shouldn't have sent her to bed with laudanum and waited to fetch the doctor. But it was only a headache. She often suffered from them. Who knew a headache could kill? If only I'd called the doctor sooner."

"You mustn't blame yourself," Miss Sheldon put a gloved hand on his arm, and her touch filled him with warmth. "It was only a headache. How were you to know?"

Oliver shook his head. "The doctor couldn't make sense of it. It was simply inexplicable. She was young, healthy, and so full of life, yet killed by a simple headache."

"I'm sorry," Miss Sheldon said. "Life can be cruel. Perhaps I am lucky to be marrying a man I could never love."

The sadness in her voice was palpable, and Oliver's heart ached for her and for himself. To deny oneself love for fear of loss suddenly seemed ludicrous. The eight years he'd spent with his wife had been the happiest of his life. Despite the pain of her loss, he could never regret the love they'd shared. "You're wrong," he said suddenly. "Don't marry that rogue Middlemarch. You deserve to love again."

She gave him a sad smile. "We had this conversation already, my lord, and I told you then that I don't have a choice."

Oliver went silent. *What do you have to lose?* The Black Widow's words came back to him. *If you truly cannot have a child of your own, then this is your chance to gain a family. To be happy again. No one will know any differently.*

"Kate." He reached and brushed a chestnut strand from her face. "What I told Mrs. Dove-Lyon—it was a mistake. If you'll permit it, I'd like to reconsider."

"Reconsider?" She took a step back as if rejecting the idea with her whole body.

"What I mean is—I'd like us to spend some time together, and if you find me agreeable—suitable—I'd like to—" he paused.

"You'd like to do what?" She cocked her head. "Propose marriage?" Her tone was incredulous and somewhat harsh.

"Perhaps?" he said, surprised by her anger. "If we find each other agreeable."

"But it's too late! I'm already betrothed."

"And I told you Middlemarch won't be a problem."

"I don't want to marry a man who pities me." She straightened her shoulders. "Middlemarch may be cruel, but at least he doesn't pity me."

"That's not—" he began.

Thank you, Lord Knox," Miss Sheldon said, cutting him off, "for your very kind offer of help. I know you mean well, and I appreciate the gesture, but I made my own choices, and now I must pay the price. Now, if you'll excuse me, I must get back before my aunt misses me. Good day, my lord," she said, rushing past him as her tears started to flow again.

Oliver stood frozen, knowing he should chase after her and insist on escorting her home, but he could not move. The silence of the early morning engulfed him as he watched her go.

"WHERE IN THE world have you been, Kate?" I have been worried sick." Aunt Jane put down her newspaper as Kate entered the breakfast room.

"Only in the park, Aunt. You needn't have worried. You know I enjoy a morning walk when I have difficulty sleeping."

"You went to the park unchaperoned? Kate, you know better than that!"

"Oh, Aunt, I have enough to worry about without concerning

myself with London gossips."

Aunt Jane's face softened. "Why have you had difficulty sleeping? Is something wrong? Is the babe—"

"No," Kate said. It's nothing like that." She poured herself a cup of tea and sat beside her aunt at the round breakfast table. "It's a lovely morning, and a walk in the fresh air did me a world of good."

"Did it?" Her aunt stirred a lump of sugar into her tea. "Because you look perturbed. I can tell you've been crying. Did something happen?"

Kate hesitated, uncertain whether or not she should tell her aunt about her meeting with the earl.

"What is it?" Her aunt pressed. "I know you, Kate. You can't hide things from me. I know something happened, and as your aunt and chaperone here in London, I demand you tell me."

Kate sighed. "It's nothing, really. I bumped into Lord Knox in the park, that's all."

"The earl?"

Kate nodded.

"The same earl that Mrs. Dove-Lyon thought would be a good match for you?"

Kate nodded again.

Her aunt pursed her lips. "Well, I'm sorry for him. He had the opportunity to be matched with a wonderful woman like you, and he chose against even meeting with you. Did he seem to know who you were?"

"He knew exactly who I was," Kate said.

"How odd." Her aunt sipped her tea.

"Not really. In fact, I've noticed him watching me at the Lyon's Den on more than one occasion. We even spoke the night of the auction."

"The night of the auction *and* this morning?"

Kate nodded.

"What did he say?"

"He suggested that he'd made a mistake telling Mrs. Dove-Lyon he wasn't interested and advised me not to marry Middlemarch."

Her aunt, who was about to take another sip of tea, froze. "He what?" she said.

"He voiced his objection to Middlemarch as a good match for me and said perhaps we should spend some time together getting acquainted."

Her aunt put her teacup down slowly. "And what did you say to that?"

"I said no, of course."

"You said no to an earl?" Her aunt reiterated as though she could not believe her own ears.

Kate dropped a lump of sugar into her teacup and sighed. "He's too late. I'm already bound to Middlemarch."

"I simply don't understand," her aunt pressed. "You've expressed your dislike for Middlemarch, and this is your chance to escape marriage to him—and to a man far more powerful. He knows about your babe, and he accepts you as you are!"

"He doesn't want to marry me," Kate said. "He feels sorry for me."

"You don't have the luxury of a second love match, Kate."

"I know that. But I'd rather enter into a loveless union than marry a man who feels sorry for me. I cannot stand to be the object of someone's pity." She shuddered at the notion that the earl's beautiful gray eyes would never burn with passion for her as Theo's had done. She'd rather endure a man she despised than endure a lifetime with a man who could never reciprocate her feelings. The realization shocked Kate, and she gasped out loud. How could she betray Theo's memory by desiring another man a mere two months after his death? What kind of a dishonorable woman was she? If she was that fickle, then she deserved her fate with Middlemarch. She'd had her chance at love, which was more than some ever got.

A flock of starlings swooped into the garden and caught Kate's eye. She got up and walked to the window just in time to see them swoop out again and watched as they soared into the sky. She sighed. Freedom really was for the birds. *They can fly free, but I must repress my fickle desires and learn to keep my mouth closed and my heart buried. It is the right thing to do, and do it I shall, no matter how difficult.*

CHAPTER SIX

SEVERAL HOURS LATER, Kate sat with her aunt in the drawing room, soaking up the last sliver of afternoon sun that filtered through the windows, which would no doubt soon vanish. She held a worn copy of *Sense and Sensibility*, a book she'd loved. She never tired of reading about the Dashwood sisters. Usually, their troubles took her mind off her own, but not today. She could not concentrate on her reading because, try as she may, she could not repress her thoughts of Lord Knox. She wanted so badly to be stoic—to honor the love she'd shared with Theo, but the more she tried to forget what had happened in the park earlier, the more persistent her doubts became. Was Aunt Jane, correct? Had she been too quick to rebuff Lord Knox—a handsome and powerful earl—and possibly the only person who could help her out of her predicament?

Papa had always said she was too proud. She'd rather condemn herself to a lifetime with a nasty and selfish little man like Middlemarch than accept that Lord Knox might never find her as devastatingly attractive as she found him. But in truth, she missed what she'd had with Theo. She wanted to feel love and passion again. Kate shuddered. She was like Eve—unable to return to her pure state after tasting the forbidden fruit.

"Miss Kathrine, there's a gentleman here to see you." The butler came into the drawing room.

"A gentleman?" Kate's heart leapt.

"Yes, miss. One Lord Middlemarch. May I show him in?"

Her heart plummeted and then started to beat rapidly. *What is Middlemarch doing here?* Had he come to tell her that he'd finally arranged the special license and was ready to set a date for their marriage? In as little as one or two days from now, she could be Lady Middlemarch. The thought made her nauseous.

She swallowed and tried to compose herself. "Certainly, Mason," she said.

Aunt Jane stood, smoothed her sky-blue dress, and placed a comforting hand on Kate's shoulder.

Seconds later, the butler reappeared and announced the arrival of Lord Middlemarch, who stepped into the room. Although it had only been a few days since Kate had last seen him, she thought he looked even more gaunt and sour than she'd remembered. Kate forced a polite smile but found she was unable to speak.

"Lord Middlemarch, how kind of you to pay us a visit," her aunt said. "Please sit down. Shall I call for tea?"

"No," he said abruptly, leaning slightly on his walking stick. "I won't be long. I have something of great importance to discuss with Miss Sheldon."

"Of great importance," her aunt repeated, raising her eyebrows. "Do you need a moment alone?"

Alone. Kate's stomach sank. That could only mean one thing. He'd secured the marriage license and wanted to set a date.

"That won't be necessary. As her chaperone, it's important that you hear what I have to say."

"Very well." Her aunt gestured again to the dark blue velvet armchair, indicating that Middlemarch should sit.

Middlemarch relented and sat on the edge of the chair, his back rigid. The two women sat on the settee opposite and looked at him expectantly. He cleared his throat. "It has come to my attention that Miss Sheldon was spotted in St. James's' Park unchaperoned while in the company of a gentleman this morning."

Kate straightened her back and looked Middlemarch directly in the eyes. "Yes, I went for a stroll in the park early this morning and bumped into Lord Knox. We exchanged a few words and then went our separate ways."

"So you admit that you went to the park unchaperoned and spent time alone with a gentleman?"

"Yes, but there was no harm done."

"You were seen. Of course, there was harm done. You are an unmarried woman, unchaperoned and alone with a gentleman. Do you suppose I shall tolerate a wife who conducts herself like a bawd?"

Aunt Jane inhaled sharply.

Heat spread across Kate's cheeks. She opened her mouth to speak, but her aunt cleared her throat loudly and said, "You are correct, my lord. Kate should not have left the house unchaperoned. On the other hand, there is no need for you to insult and disrespect her in such a manner."

Middlemarch's features hardened. "Insult her? It is she who insults and disrespects me with her conduct. If she is to be my wife, then—"

"*If*, my lord? Aunt Jane said pointedly.

"*When* Kate learns to respect me." Middlemarch said through gritted teeth. Then he turned to Kate. "I want you to stay indoors. You may no longer venture outdoors for more than one hour a day. And you must be chaperoned at all times. Is that understood?"

Kate's chest flamed. Middlemarch had gone too far in trying to lock her up. She could not marry him—she would not do it!

"You're too late," she blurted.

"What?" Middlemarch narrowed his eyes.

"I can no longer marry you because I accepted Lord Knox's proposal this morning." Kate's heartbeat accelerated. She could not believe the words that had just come out of her mouth!

"You what? That's impossible. You are betrothed to me! We have a contract!"

He was right, of course. She'd entered the auction with her eyes open. And she'd agreed to marry the highest bidder. But Lord Knox's words gave her courage. *Middlemarch won't be a problem.* She squared her shoulders. "I'm breaking the contract," she said calmly. "I'm sorry, Lord Middlemarch, but I don't think we are a good match."

"No one asked you to think. Your job is to look pleasant, and do as I say," he snarled. "You belong to me! I paid good money for you!"

Kate gritted her teeth, forcing herself to remain calm. It would do no good to give him the satisfaction of upsetting her. "No matter," she said. "I'm marrying the Earl of Knox, and not you."

Middlemarch's lips curved into an ugly smirk. "We shall see about that."

He turned and strode furiously toward the door, pausing as he passed the blue and white porcelain vase filled with flowers perched on a small table. He lifted his walking stick and swatted the vase as though it were a cricket ball. The fragile glass shattered on impact, sending water, petals, and blue and white shards through the air.

Kate gasped, but Middlemarch did not even turn around. He continued his furious walk and exited the room.

Chapter Seven

Kate and her aunt stared in shock at the shattered mess on the floor.

"How dare he?" Aunt Jane fumed. "Who does he think he is coming into my home and behaving in such a boorish manner?"

"I don't know what came over me!" Kate paced back and forth. "What am I to do now? What will Lord Knox think?"

"Why should he think anything? You said he regretted his decision and urged you not to marry Middlemarch?"

"That's true. He expressed his regret for the hasty rejection and suggested we spend time together—to see if we found each other agreeable. But that's not the same as a formal proposal."

"But it's a promise of sorts. An honorable man doesn't tell a woman to leave her betrothed and spend time with him unless he intends to marry her."

"But I rebuffed him! And now I have announced our betrothal!" She clasped her face in her hands. "What will he think when Middlemarch approaches him—or worse, complains to Mrs. Dove-Lyon and tells her that Lord Knox is responsible for my having broken our contract?"

"Yes, that is a conundrum." Aunt Jane frowned and massaged her forehead as she often did when troubled. "We must speak with Mrs. Dove-Lyon before Middlemarch does," she said, looking up at Kate. "I think he will approach Lord Knox first. That's what angry men do—they confront their rivals in love. He'll do that before running to Mrs. Dove-Lyon."

"Not Middlemarch. I suspect he is a coward who only likes to bully women, children, and servants." Kate put a protective hand on her stomach. "And Lord Knox is twice his size."

"Perhaps you're right, and I'm proud of you for standing up to him. I'm sorry I didn't listen when you first voiced your doubts. But you needn't worry. After today, I cannot allow you to marry that man."

Kate nodded. Her breathing eased a little, but her insides still trembled. Freedom was within reach.

"Come along, Kate," Aunt Jane said, "let's get our hats and coats. We must leave at once."

KATE WAS SURPRISED when the tall, broad-shouldered Hermia greeted them at the women's entrance of the Lyon's Den, saying, "Aah, Mrs. Seton, Miss Sheldon, you're right on time. Mrs. Dove-Lyon is waiting for you in her office."

Kate and her aunt shared a glance, each realizing that Middlemarch must already be in Mrs. Dove-Lyon's office, airing his grievances. A tight knot formed in Kate's stomach as they followed Hermia along the marbled floor, softened by a plush red and gold patterned runner that worked its way up the staircase.

She'd heard people say that it was a mistake to cross the Black

Widow of Whitehall. What did she do to those who broke contracts with her? Kate gave an involuntary shudder as they approached Mrs. Dove-Lyon's office. What if the widow forced her to honor the contract and marry Middlemarch?

When Hermia opened the door, Kate froze. Lord Middlemarch sat in one of the elegant scarlet chairs facing Mrs. Dove-Lyon's desk. His cravat hung loose, and his shirt and hair were disheveled. A purple bruise marred his eye, and he held a handkerchief to his blood-clotted nose. Theseus, Mrs. Dove-Lyon's wolf, stood behind Middlemarch, his large muscular arms folded and his face stony.

The situation had obviously gotten volatile quickly. She'd underestimated Middlemarch. He wasn't simply a bully. He was also a fool.

"Mrs. Seton, Miss Sheldon, we've been waiting for you." The Black Widow pushed back her desk chair and stood up. "Now that you are here, let's all move to the seating area where we will have more space to discuss what has unfolded."

Mrs. Dove-Lyon led them to a seating area where a plush scarlet settee with carved mahogany legs, the feet of which were shaped into lion claws, and three matching chairs were arranged around an oval tea table upon which a silver tray sat. Theseus stayed close to Middlemarch as he moved to the seating area and sat down. Once the baron was seated, Theseus planted himself firmly behind Middlemarch's armchair.

The knot in Kate's stomach tightened as she realized he was keeping Middlemarch under control. But what exactly had Middlemarch done?

As if in answer to her question, the door opened, and Hermia showed Lord Knox inside. Kate gasped at the sight of him. Like Middlemarch his hair and clothing were disheveled. His white shirt sat open at the neck and rolled up at the sleeves. Cuts and scrapes marred his knuckles, and a small bruise had formed on the apple of his right cheek. Kate's pulse raced and her stomach fluttered. How could someone look so beautiful and vulnerable at the same time? It was easy to guess what happened. Middlemarch had confronted Lord Knox, and they'd probably engaged in fisticuffs. They'd been fighting over her! It must have been broken up by Theseus, who'd brought them to Mrs. Dove-Lyon to air their grievances. That's how she knew Kate and her aunt would likely be arriving. She wanted to jump up, take him in her arms, treat his wounds, and kiss him all at once.

As Lord Knox neared, Kate saw the fury on his face and quickly averted her gaze as he sat in one of the armchairs adjacent to her. She felt Lord Knox's eyes on her, but she couldn't bring herself to look at him. What must he think of her for dragging him into this mess—especially when she'd so haughtily rebuffed his offer of help?

Mrs. Dove-Lyon busied herself pouring tea while Lord Knox got himself settled, and Kate accepted a teacup with a shaky hand.

"Now," Mrs. Dove-Lyon said from behind her black veil, "as you ladies well know, there seems to be a misunderstanding concerning Miss Sheldon, Lord Middlemarch, and Lord Knox, which resulted in an altercation in my club."

Kate shifted in her seat. So, Middlemarch had confronted Lord Knox at the club.

Last time we spoke, Lord Knox, you expressed no interest in remarrying. Can you explain Miss Sheldon's claim that you have proposed to her?"

Nausea took hold of Kate. She was keenly aware of Lord Knox sitting on the armchair to her left, but she dared not look at him. Just the thought of what she'd done made her cheeks flame. How would she explain herself? Accepting a proposal from a man who'd not actually proposed? She tried to open her mouth to speak but found it impossible. There was nothing she *could* say.

Lord Knox cleared his throat, and she squeezed her eyes shut. "Soon after our conversation, I realized I'd made a mistake refusing your offer to meet with Miss Sheldon. My hesitation stemmed from my own fears and doubts. But upon observing Miss Sheldon, I understood that I'd be foolish to throw away the opportunity to"—he paused—" to know such a lovely and gracious young lady."

Kate's stomach somersaulted. She'd been staring into her teacup to avoid looking at Lord Knox, but she pressed her lips together to suppress her smile upon hearing his words.

"You only decided that you desired Miss Sheldon after you learned that she belonged to me! I paid for her!" Middlemarch started out of his chair, but Theseus placed his large hand on the baron's shoulder, forcing him back down.

Kate could take no more. "I belong to no one but myself," she snapped. She'd heard him make that claim one too many times, and she could no longer keep silent. "I'm a woman, not your horse."

"Bravo!" Aunt Jane chimed.

"That's not what our contract states," Middlemarch said.

"Lord Middlemarch is correct in reminding us that a legal contract is a serious commitment and not something to be taken lightly." Mrs. Dove-Lyon's words silenced the room.

Kate's heart sank. She was going to force her to honor the contract and marry Middlemarch.

"Violating a contract with me is a serious affront."

Kate swallowed the lump of fear in her throat.

"Theseus," Mrs. Dove-Lyon said.

Theseus reached into his jacket pocket and brought out a folded piece of paper, which he handed to Mrs. Dove-Lyon.

Kate bit her lip as she watched the Black Widow unfold the paper and scan the document. "Just as I thought." She handed the paper to Middlemarch, and Kate glimpsed the Black Widow's gold lion seal at the bottom of the page.

A satisfied smirk appeared on Middlemarch's face as soon as he held the document. The sight made Kate even sicker to her stomach.

"Let me draw your attention to the final paragraph, Lord Middlemarch," Mrs. Dove Lyon said.

"Please do," Middlemarch said with an air of superiority that Kate found repulsive.

"Would you care to read it out loud, so we all can hear what it says?"

"Certainly," Middlemarch smirked, straightening his posture, and looking directly at Kate as if to say, *I warned you.*

"Lord Middlemarch agrees to keep both his and Miss Sheldon's participation in the auction a secret until they are wed." Middlemarch read. "He further agrees to obtain a special license and marry Miss Kathrine Sheldon within two days of signing this document, or he shall…What is this?" Middlemarch demanded.

"Keep reading," Mrs. Dove-Lyon said calmly.

Middlemarch returned to the document and continued, "Or he shall forfeit any claim he has on Miss Sheldon."

All the heaviness that had been weighing Kate down, suddenly lifted from her body.

"This is preposterous," Middlemarch slammed the document onto the table, and Theseus's large hand immediately came down on his shoulder.

"It's the contract you signed," Mrs. Dove-Lyon's voice was like ice. "And by signing it you agreed to abide by the conditions set forth, which you failed to do on two counts. First, you told Lord Knox that you had won the auction and that your prize was Miss Sheldon, and second, you failed to obtain a license and marry within two days."

"You tricked me!" he said. "Who marries two days after betrothal? A wedding takes planning."

"There was no trickery involved. The rules were clearly stipulated on paper. Perhaps, Lord Middlemarch, you might consider reading a document before you sign it next time." The contempt in Mrs. Dove-Lyon's voice was palpable.

"What about the money? I paid one-hundred-and-forty pounds for her. She has to marry me."

"She need do no such thing," Mrs. Dove-Lyon roared. "Not only did you violate the conditions of the contract, but you compromised her reputation. Those stipulations were put in place to secure her honor and future. But it seems you were more interested in playing cruel games than entering a serious marriage. Therefore, Miss Sheldon owes you nothing."

Middlemarch shrank back into his chair.

"And as for me, you forfeited your invitation to the club when you broke confidentiality by sharing information about the auction and then came into my establishment swinging your fists and accosting one of my patrons!"

"But—" Middlemarch objected.

"You can be grateful that you only told Lord Knox—a man of immense integrity and trustworthiness—about the auction, or your punishment would have been more severe." The Black Widow turned to her wolf "Theseus, show Lord Middlemarch out. He is henceforth barred from entering this club."

"Don't touch me!" Middlemarch stood and tossed his head haughtily. "I will be more than happy to be rid of her and the lot of you. I will show myself out!"

Kate and the rest of the widow's guests watched in silence as a red-faced Middlemarch strode out of the office with Theseus following close behind. Kate listened to hear for any breaking glass, but apparently the odious man had enough sense not to break any of the Black Widow's vases.

"Now," Mrs. Dove-Lyon turned to Lord Knox, "Before we have any more mishaps, let's be clear. "Do you intend to marry Miss Sheldon?"

Kate held her breath as she watched Lord Knox hesitate. Heat flooded her cheeks. She could not just sit back and force this man into a marriage based on a lie. "This is all my doing. He never promised me marriage. I only said that to—"

"I do," Lord Knox interjected, gently reaching for her hand. She stopped mid-sentence and turned to him. His gray eyes met her gaze, and stomach turned to jelly. "I meant what I said, I want you to be my wife."

A cascade of mixed emotions flooded Kate. She was both elated and fearful. Had she forced this upon Lord Knox? He'd only wanted to help, and now he was committing to her for life.

"Miss Sheldon?" The widow turned to her. "Do you agree to marry Lord Knox? And before you answer, let me just say, I think you would be a fool to refuse him."

Kate blinked. Her heart said yes, but her voice could not project the words. She nodded.

"Excellent!" Mrs. Dove-Lyon clapped her hands, breaking the intimacy of the moment. "We all know the urgency of this situation, so I expect you will obtain the special license and marry immediately." She stood. "My work is now complete. I expect the two of you will want a few minutes alone, so I'll leave you." She turned to Aunt Jane, "Will you join me in the gaming room, Mrs. Seton?"

"Certainly." Aunt Jane stood and gave Kate a beaming smile as she left the room with Mrs. Dove-Lyon.

"I'M SORRY," KATE said as soon as the women were out of earshot. "I didn't mean to force this marriage upon you. I'll find a way to make this right. I'll explain what happened—"

"Stop." Oliver moved from his armchair onto the sofa next to Kate and took hold of her gloved hands. "You don't need to explain because you didn't force me into anything."

Kate's cheeks flushed. "Of course I did, my lord. You hardly even know me. All you did was show me a bit of kindness and the next thing you're—"

"Don't call me 'my lord,'" Oliver murmured, shifting closer, desperate to close the gap between them. "I'm to be your husband, so I'm Oliver to you."

She gazed at him, devouring his face with her beautiful, soulful dark eyes. He felt certain that she wanted him as much as he wanted her. Then she dropped her gaze and shook her head.

"Kate," he whispered, reaching out to lightly caress the back of her neck. He wished she would just let him love her.

She breathed steadily as he leaned forward and brushed her skin with his lips.

"No," she said, moving back suddenly. "I cannot let you marry me out of pity or because you feel the need to save me from a worse marriage. I admire you too much to let you make such a sacrifice."

Oliver gently squeezed her hand. How could he make her understand? "Kate, listen to me. The reason I want to marry you is entirely selfish. It has nothing to do with pitying you."

She stopped her protest and gave him her full attention. Oliver released her hands and straightened his shoulders, preparing himself to reveal what was most painful to him. He told her about his wife and her lost child, confessing that he'd been unable to give her another. And then, looking directly into Kate's eyes, he told her what was now in his heart, "Since losing Beatrice, I have been alone. And I was prepared to stay that way. Until I met you. Now the hope of having a family is real."

Kate put her hands on her stomach. "You want me for my child?" she said, hesitantly.

"No, Kate. I want you *and* your child. Your loyalty, courage, and love for your unborn babe is something I admire greatly—a quality I will cherish in a wife. I want the three of us to make a new and happy family together."

"And you will love him like your own?"

"Or her, yes. I will be your child's father in name and heart, and no one need know any differently. If it's a boy, he will inherit my title, and if it's a girl, she shall have all the advantages and protections of an earl's daughter."

A dimple appeared on Kate's cheek as her lips spread into a smile.

Oliver slipped out of his chair and knelt before Kate, clasping her hands in his once again. "Kate, you have a fighting spirit, a loving, loyal heart, and a beauty that takes my breath away. What more can a man ask for? I want to wake up beside you every day for the rest of my life. Do you understand?"

Kate bit her bottom lip and nodded, tears pooling in her eyes.

"Then answer me this. Miss Katherine Sheldon, will you marry me?"

"I will," Kate's eyes shone with tears. "I will."

"Then there is only one thing left to do," Oliver said, slipping his arms around Kate's still-slim waist and pressing his lips to hers.

Chapter Eight

One Month Later

THAT FIRST KISS changed everything for Kate. She'd never thought she could feel such an intense passion for anyone besides Theo. Yet, her love for Oliver was even greater, if possible. His kisses were far more tender than Theo's had been. Oliver took his time exploring her mouth and letting her explore his—their urgency and desire building together.

Theo's kisses had been shorter as if he wanted to hurry and focus on the other more interesting areas of her body. She now felt like an impatient girl for having been swept up in his sweet words and the overwhelming urgency of the situation.

But after taking care of her sisters and father for seven years and never being allowed to debut into society, she'd been starved for excitement and passion. She'd desperately wanted to get married, but her father would never have allowed a man to court her. So when she met Theo after befriending his sister Emilia, it had seemed like a dream come true. Here was a man who loved her enough to confront her father, to marry her even if Papa disapproved, and to take her away from the life of drudgery that awaited her once her little sisters married, and she was left to care for her father in his dotage.

But that was her old life. Kate smiled at her sleeping husband, who lay beside her. They'd married a week ago in a chapel on St. James's Street. Everything had been done in a secret rush, with only Kate's aunt and a second witness from the church in attendance as witnesses.

Her papa had only been informed after the fact. There had been no time to invite him—she didn't need his permission, nor did she fear his reaction, knowing that he might be cross at first, but also realizing that once he digested the fact that she'd married an earl, he'd be elated.

Aunt Jane had traveled back to Yorkshire directly after the wedding to break the news to her brother-in-law, but the journey up north was long, so Kate had written to her papa as soon as Oliver had secured the special license, knowing that once word got out that the Earl of Knox had secretly married again, the news would spread as fast as a row of thatched huts on fire. And it had.

But Kate didn't care to know what people were saying. She and Oliver had cocooned themselves in his home, shutting out the rest of the world. Although she'd been hesitant at first, and they hadn't had much time for courtship, Oliver now felt like her soulmate. They'd quickly developed a deep friendship, respect, and love for one another in and out of the bedroom.

At first, Kate had been worried about being intimate with her husband because of the baby. Could marital relations hurt her unborn child? But she needn't have worried because Oliver had been the most gentle and considerate lover. And once that initial fear had passed, they couldn't get enough of one another, spending their nights—and much of their days—making love.

Now, Oliver's eyes fluttered open, and he smiled at his wife. Kate moved into his arms, pressing her naked body against his. He lifted her chin and pressed his lips to hers, opening his mouth and kissing her deeply. She returned his kiss and let her hand travel over his muscular chest and down between his thighs. He groaned and lifted her onto his manhood. They moved their hips back and forth until waves of pleasure engulfed both of them, and they cried out from pleasure. Afterward, Kate lay on his chest with him still inside her, neither wanting to separate. They stayed that way for several minutes until Kate eventually rolled over.

"I'm starving," she said.

Oliver laughed, threw off the blankets, and sat up. "I'll tell Cook to prepare you a feast fit for a queen. What do you fancy? Eggs, kippers, and bacon? What about toast and marmalade? I could use a steaming cup of tea myself."

"All of the above," Kate said.

"Good. You get ready, and by the time you come downstairs, a feast will be waiting."

"Aren't we going to breakfast together?" Kate asked.

"I'm afraid I'll have to leave you for a bit today and retreat to my study. I have some matters to attend to. And I expect you do, too."

"What do you mean?" Kate pushed herself up on her elbows.

"We can't stay holed up in this house forever. Your father will be expecting an invitation to visit, and we'll have to make our appearance in society next week at Lady Ashworth's ball. I expect you'll want some new dresses, so you'll need to summon the modiste."

Kate groaned. "Can't we spend another week alone before we start doing all of those things?"

"I'd like nothing better, my darling," Oliver said, "but I'm afraid not."

"Will you at least have a little breakfast with me before you retreat?" Kate asked.

Oliver looked at his wife and smiled. "Of course, I will. Today and every other day," He leaned over to give her another kiss. She returned his kiss, wrapping her arms around his muscular back and pulling him down to her. His desire pressed against her soft flesh, and he groaned. "Perhaps my work can wait just a little longer," he said, kissing her again.

Kate spent the next week getting measured and choosing fabric for her new dresses. The modiste had promised to have one ready for Kate's first public appearance with Oliver at Lady Ashworth's ball, and she'd delivered a stunning royal blue satin empire dress with a square neckline, puffed sleeves, and a red sash covering the high waist. She finished the outfit with red silk slippers and a diamond-encrusted ruby necklace and earrings that Oliver had given to her as a wedding gift. Her chestnut curls had been pulled and twisted into a bun by her lady's maid, who artfully arranged ringlets to frame her face.

"You look radiant, m'lady."

"Thank you, Elspeth. It isn't too difficult when you have so many wonderful people looking after you, doing your hair, and sewing beautiful dresses for you." Kate studied herself in the oval full-length floor mirror, looking for signs of her being with child. She turned to the side and saw no visible bump. Her waist was still slim.

"I'd wager you'd look radiant even if you wore rags, m'lady. There's just something that glows about your face."

Kate swallowed. She wondered what her maid was hinting at. Had she guessed that she was with child? Kate had heard that women could sometimes sense these things about each other, but her lady's maid had no children of her own, so Kate decided it was unlikely the woman could tell.

"But I suppose it's because you're so happy. His lordship is just the same. All the servants have noticed how much he's changed since my old mistress died. We never thought he'd be happy again, and then you came along."

"*Your* old mistress?" Kate asked, suddenly curious as to why Oliver had retained his wife's lady's maid.

"Lord Knox didn't have the heart to let me go. He's an awfully generous master, he is, and he knew how loyal I was to Lady Knox, so he kept me on as a housemaid. It was a bit of a demotion for me, but he kept my wages the same, so I stayed, and I'm glad I did because now all is right in this household again."

Just then Oliver entered the room, looking dashing in his three-piece navy suit with a red and navy patterned waistcoat over his white shirt.

"That will be all, thank you, Elspeth," Kate said.

Elspeth curtsied and said, "Yes, m'lady," before exiting the room.

Oliver came up behind Kate and kissed her neck. "You smell delicious," he said, "and look stunning. I'm going to be the envy of every man tonight."

Kate laughed and turned to face her husband. "Hardly, I think I am the one who will receive envious stares from all the women."

"Well then, why don't we go and find out, Lady Knox," Oliver said.

"The Earl of Knox and Lady Knox," the doorman announced as they stepped into Lady Ashworth's ballroom, and Kate saw many heads turn to look in their direction. Oliver squeezed Kate's arm lightly in a reassuring gesture. Despite being a baronet's daughter, she'd spent her life in Yorkshire and had never made her debut into society, so she'd had little experience attending balls and mingling with the ton. But she needn't have worried because Oliver stayed closely by her side, introducing her to the host and others who came to greet them. Kate smiled at so many people that her cheeks began to ache.

"Who knew smiling and making small talk with people was so exhausting," she said.

"Oh, believe me, it's a marathon," Oliver said. "If you want to go, I can make our excuses. I don't want you to over-exert yourself."

"Nonsense," Kate said. "We only just got here, and we haven't even danced yet. I spent years learning to dance and then never had a chance to put my lessons into practice."

"Well then, may I have this dance, my lady?"

"I don't know," Kate teased, holding out her wrist and pretending to read an imaginary dance card. "It looks like my card is full. I'm afraid you'll have to wait until the next ball."

"Forget them," he said, taking her hand and starting for the ballroom floor. "I'll duel every one of them to the death if I have to."

Kate giggled as Oliver grabbed her waist and twirled her onto the ballroom floor. Then she realized that heads had turned, and they were attracting attention. She straightened and turned back to Oliver, trying to appear somber.

"People are looking at us," she said.

"Let them," Oliver said. "I want the whole world to know how happy you make me."

The music started, and she glided across the ballroom floor with her husband. How wonderful it felt to be dancing. But after three dances, Kate had to excuse herself to go to the withdrawing room, so Oliver escorted her off the floor.

"I'll fetch you a glass of iced tea in the meantime," he said.

"That would be lovely."

As Kate weaved her way through the crowded room toward the exit, a young woman, standing in a far-off corner, sipping a glass of champagne, caught her eye. She wore a yellow empire dress with a white sash. Kate's heart began to pound. There was something familiar about her tall, slim physique, and the way she wore her blond hair in an elaborate bun.

"Emilia," she whispered.

As though the young woman sensed a presence calling out to her, she turned and gazed into the crowded room.

"Emilia," Kate whispered again, advancing cautiously. As she got closer, her knees almost gave way. There was no mistaking those ice blue eyes and sharp cheekbones.

A mad desperation gripped Kate. *Am I hallucinating? Emilia is dead! Yet, here she stands before me as she did in life.*

Kate pushed forward, weaving through the crowd. She needed to touch Emilia, feel her warmth and know that she wasn't going mad. But when she reached the spot where Emilia had stood, there was no sign of her friend.

Kate blinked at the space where Emilia had stood, sipping champagne in her yellow gown. She cradled her head in her hands. What had happened? Had her mind played a trick on her? Emilia was dead. She knew that. Yet, she could have sworn…

Kate's body trembled, and a heavy weight settled on her chest, making it hard to breathe. Emilia had looked so real—so alive. Those eyes and that beautiful face—she'd know it anywhere. What was happening to her?

Oh, Emilia, why do you haunt me now? Is it because I betrayed your brother by falling in love again so soon? Tears stung Kate's eyes, as she realized that it must have been her guilty mind at work. So much had happened since Theo's and Emilia's deaths that she'd hardly had time to mourn them properly. And here she was at an elaborate ball, laughing and dancing with her new husband as though Theo had never existed.

"Kate." Oliver appeared by her side. "What happened? I've been searching everywhere for you. Why do you tremble so? Are you cold?"

Kate shook her head. She couldn't tell Oliver what she'd seen. He would think her mad and worry himself sick. "I—I don't know. I suddenly felt nauseated."

"Good Lord." Oliver removed his jacket and put it around his wife's shoulders. "I should not have pushed you to attend this ball. I'm a fool. You are with child. You need your rest." He wrapped his arms around her. "Forgive me."

Kate burrowed against his chest, taking comfort in his warmth and leather and spice scent. Her body relaxed. She desired sleep. Her exhaustion had caused her to become confused. That was all.

I am with child. I need my rest. All will be well with a little sleep.

Chapter Nine

OLIVER WAS WORRIED. He'd only left Kate's side for a few minutes the previous evening, and she'd somehow ended up in a corner, looking pale and extremely ill. One minute she'd been laughing and joyful, and the next, he'd found her across the room, shaking like a leaf in the autumn wind. She'd denied anything had happened—no one had accosted or frightened her—she'd merely suffered an attack of nausea. It was a normal part of being with child. He'd taken her home at once and given her a tiny drop of laudanum so that she could rest. And he'd called the doctor in the morning, who'd determined that Kate was suffering from exhaustion. Was he to blame? The constant lovemaking since their marriage, the rush and bustle of choosing a new wardrobe, and the stress of being introduced to society as the new Lady Knox. Why had he pushed her so?

With adequate rest, all will be well. There is no need to fret. The doctor had reassured him. Still, he could not help but worry. The incident had brought up painful memories of the past. And he would not survive another loss. He'd finally opened his heart again, and he couldn't believe how much his life had changed. He had a beautiful wife, and in a few months, he would be a father. The house would be filled with laughter and joy. But every love came with risk, and now he wondered if the risk had been worth taking. If only Kate's aunt hadn't returned to Yorkshire. Perhaps, he should send for her again. Kate needed someone—another woman—to watch over her while he was working.

Oliver sat behind his desk and dropped his head in his hands. He had work that needed his attention, but he could not concentrate. His mind kept wandering back to Kate.

A short rap on Oliver's office door sounded. "Enter," Oliver said. Normally, he didn't like to be disturbed while working, but he'd made himself fully available lest Kate needed him.

The door opened to reveal his butler, Moses, in the doorway. "There's a young lady here who claims to be your cousin, my lord," Moses said in his pinched, nasal tone.

"My cousin?" Oliver frowned.

"Yes, my lord. She says her name is Emilia Harrington—the sister of one Mathew James Harrington, your deceased heir."

Oliver's frown deepened. How odd. He hadn't even known that Harrington had had a sister. But of course, it was probable. He wondered what she wanted from him.

"Shall I tell her to wait, my lord?"

"No," Oliver said, curious now. "Show her to my office."

The butler withdrew and Oliver rubbed the worry from his face and ran a hand through his disheveled hair. Then he cleared his throat and sat up straight, awaiting his guest. Oliver stood as the young woman entered his office dressed in black mourning attire. She was a beautiful woman—tall and slim with white-blond hair and icy blue eyes. Oliver thought she looked oddly familiar. But he could not place her.

"Miss Harrington," Oliver said. "This is a surprise."

"Thank you for agreeing to see me, my lord."

"Of course," Oliver said, inviting her to sit. "Forgive me for asking this, but have we met before?"

"No, my lord. I would have remembered if I'd been introduced to my own cousin."

"Yes, of course. Forgive me." Oliver grinned sheepishly. "Tell me, how can I help you?"

"As you know, my brother, your heir, was killed in a carriage accident two months ago."

"Yes, I was truly sorry to receive the news of his death."

"What you may not know is that I was in the carriage with him that day."

"No. I only received news of your brother's death. I wasn't informed about the details of the crash. I hope you didn't suffer any serious injuries."

"I was extremely lucky. We were both thrown several feet into the air when the carriage overturned and tumbled down a deep ravine. It was smashed to pieces, destroyed beyond recognition. Mathew"—she cleared her throat—"unfortunately, Mathew was killed instantly. I was knocked unconscious but miraculously survived without any broken bones. I believe it took several hours before anyone discovered our carriage as we were traveling in a rather rural area."

"Good Lord! How awful."

"Although I have no recollection of walking away from the accident site and stumbling along a country road, I am told that is what happened," Miss Harrington continued. "Luckily, a farmer and his wife driving by in their cart spotted me in my confused, bloodied state. They took me home and spent several weeks nursing me back to health. When the wreckage was eventually found, Mathew's mangled body was barely recognizable. But the constable found some of our belongings. My bloodied shawl lay at the scene, along with some of Mathew's papers, which contained his details and our Yorkshire address. We'd been renting a house there after returning from several years on the continent."

"Yes, I was told as much."

"It was from those papers that they were able to identify Mathew. And based on my bloodied shawl, the constable assumed that his companion, me, had been taken by wild animals. He went to our Yorkshire address and met with the landlord who told him that Mathew had lived with his sister, Miss Emilia Harrington. Based on that information and my bloodied shawl found at the scene, the constable declared me dead alongside my brother."

"Do you mean to say the farmer and his wife carted you away without alerting anyone that you were still alive?"

Emilia nodded. "The kind individuals who saved my life were elderly and reclusive. I said nothing to them about my brother because, at first, I couldn't remember anything, not even so much as my name. I think because of the impact on my head. Fortunately, that only lasted a few weeks, and eventually I regained my memory and strength and made my way back to Yorkshire. The landlord had all of our belongings, which I suspect he would have sold had it not been for this." She pulled a folded letter out of his pocket and handed it to Oliver.

Dear Mr. Harrington,

After thorough and extensive research, we have discovered that you are the 6th cousin of one

Oliver Henry Harrington, 4th Earl of Knox, and next in line to inherit his title and estate should he have no sons of his own. As such, we would like to meet with you as soon as possible. Please contact us by replying to this letter or by paying us a visit at the offices of Huxley and Bailey, 79 Fleet Street, London.

Yours sincerely,
Huxley and Bailey
Solicitors at Law

Oliver put down the letter.

"The landlord said he was going to write to you so you could take possession our belongings since he wasn't able to locate any other family members. And that is how I discovered that I wasn't alone in the world. I had—have—a cousin."

"I'm pleased to hear that you are, indeed, alive and well, Miss Harrington, and, of course, I am terribly sorry about your brother. If I remember correctly, your parents died when you were young?"

"Yes, Mathew was sixteen and I fourteen. Ever since then, I've relied on him to take care of me. Now that he is dead, I have nothing—no money, no home, and no family—except for you."

"Your brother didn't leave you any money?"

"My brother didn't have any money. Our father gambled everything away, and unfortunately, Mathew suffered from the same problem."

"I see."

"But we learned to fend for ourselves," she said. "And now that my brother is dead, I must do whatever it takes to secure my future."

"If I am indeed your only family, I am obliged to help you. I believe I can arrange a safe place for you to stay and perhaps give you a small allowance. My lawyers will want to verify your identity before they arrange anything—I am sure you understand."

"I believe your wife, Kate, can do that for you."

"My wife?" Oliver said. "How do know—"

Miss Harrington cocked her head. "Do you not know? Kate was betrothed to my brother—your heir."

Oliver felt the blood drain from his face. "What are you talking about?"

"Before my brother's death, he proposed marriage to a young lady, who also happened to be a dear friend of mine. They were very much in love, and I'm afraid they were rather careless and foolish with their passion. By that I mean, they expressed their love for one another fully—in a marital sense—before marriage. The young lady in question informed my brother that she was with child, and he proposed. She knew my brother by his childhood nickname, Theo. And her name is Katherine Sheldon, daughter of Sir Henry Sheldon of Yorkshire. So, you see, the babe your wife is carrying is my brother's child."

Oliver couldn't believe his ears. "That's ridiculous. If my wife had previously been betrothed to a Harrington, I think she would have told me as much."

"She wouldn't have known. Theo and I despised my father. He was a drunk and a gambler whose reputation preceded him, so we often used our mother's maiden name, Thurston."

Oliver clasped his hands together. "You're telling me that my wife was betrothed to a man who used a false name?"

"They were secretly betrothed. And he didn't use a false name. As I said, Theo was his childhood nickname; he preferred it to Mathew because that was our father's name. For that same reason, we preferred to use our mother's surname."

Oliver shook his head. "I'm sorry, but this is all sounding a bit too strange."

"Didn't your lawyers tell you anything about your heir and his parentage?"

They had, but truth be told, Oliver hadn't paid much attention. He'd still been too lost in the fog of grief to care. "One moment," he said and bent to open his bottom desk drawer from which he extracted a roll of papers tied together with string. He removed the string, unraveled the documents, and scanned the letter from his lawyers for the details he wanted.

Your sixth cousin, Mathew James Harrington, born 1790, only son of Mathew Frances Harrington (died 1799) and Mary Jane Thurston (died 1802).

Oliver lowered the document. "It doesn't say anything about Mr. Harrington having a sister in here."

"That's because women aren't important. We cannot inherit titles or entailed estates, so we are not worth mentioning. Why do you think I am here today, appealing for your help?"

She was right. His lawyers had not even bothered to tell him that his heir had a sister, nor had he cared to ask. Yet, here she sat, all alone in the world.

"Surely, Katherine told you that her babe's father died in a carriage accident and that his sister—her best friend—died alongside him. Perhaps, she even mentioned my name." Emilia raised her eyebrows.

Oliver's blood ran cold. Kate had mentioned that Theo's sister, her dearest friend, had died in the carriage accident too. But it was a painful subject and one they'd avoided talking about in their short time together. They'd tried hard to put their grief and their pasts behind them as they focused on their future.

"Well?" Emilia said.

Oliver cleared his throat. "Yes, she talked of losing her dear friend—Theo's sister—but the subject caused her so much pain, we rarely spoke of it."

"It's truly a miracle I survived. She will be overjoyed to know that I am alive and that we can be sisters once again."

Oliver didn't know what to think. He felt an implied threat in that this woman knew about Kate's babe. But, if she really was Kate's dear friend and her babe's aunt, then she would be a great comfort to Kate. All he wanted was Kate's happiness, and if Emilia contributed to her happiness, then she could stay if she wished.

KATE'S EYES FLUTTERED open. Sunlight filtered through the drawn blue velvet curtains of her bedroom. She squinted. How long had she been sleeping? Then, remembering the events from the night before, she suddenly felt very foolish. She'd been so frightened yesterday after "seeing" Emilia, thinking that she'd returned from the dead to haunt her. How silly she'd behaved. What must Oliver think after finding her in such a confused state? Still, the memory made her shudder. Her mind had played a terrible trick on her—and she'd felt the pain of losing Theo and Emilia all over again like a thousand knife wounds sent to remind her of their fate while she danced and laughed the night away.

She pushed herself into a sitting position and rubbed her eyes. Then she smiled. Oliver was standing by the door, watching her.

He strolled toward her, grinning. "Has anyone ever told you how beautiful you look when you sleep?"

Kate laughed. "Yes, you, every morning." How lucky she was to have such a dashing and adoring husband. She should not feel guilty for loving him.

Oliver sat on the bed beside her and kissed her cheek. "Are you feeling rested?"

"Yes, I feel much better," Kate said honestly.

"Good, because I have a surprise for you. One that might shock you but will bring you much joy."

"A surprise!" Kate's heart swelled. Oliver was too good to her. "What is it?"

"Not what—who," Oliver said. "She's someone you once loved dearly—someone from your past who—"

"Hello, Kate!" Emilia entered the room, cutting Oliver off mid-sentence.

Kate felt the color drain from her face. "Emilia!" She began to tremble. Was she hallucinating again? She appealed to Oliver with her eyes. *Am I going mad? Do you see her too?*

"I thought we agreed that you should wait until I called you into the room," Oliver turned to Emilia.

He's talking to her. He can see her!

"How could I possibly wait another second to see my dearest sister again!" Emilia came forward and threw her arms around Kate. "It's me, Kate. I'm alive."

"How is it possible?" Kate asked, clinging to her friend. She embraced the evidence of Emilia's warm body and familiar rose scent. This was no hallucination or dream. Emilia was alive!

"I've just explained it all to your husband. It's truly a miraculous story." They released their grip on each other.

Oliver stood up. "I'm going to leave you two alone, but I'll be back to check on you soon. If you need me before then, I'll be in my study." He looked from Emilia to Kate and smiled. "It warms my heart to see you so happy." He took Kate's hand and kissed it. "I'm right here if you need me, darling," he said and exited the room.

"I can hardly believe this," Kate said, still in shock as Emilia sat on the bed and proceeded to explain everything.

"It's a miracle," Kate repeated for the third time when Emilia finished her story. "Last night, when I saw you at the party, I thought I was hallucinating. Did you not see me, dearest? Why didn't you approach me then?"

"The party? What party? I just arrived in London this morning. And I only came here to find you, not to attend balls."

Kate froze. "But I'm certain I saw you last night at Lady Ashwood's ball."

"Who is Lady Ashwood? Did you talk to this 'Emilia' you thought you saw?"

"I tried—I called out to you, but you seemed not to hear me, so I walked to where you were standing, but when I got there, you'd disappeared." Kate rubbed her forehead. "You were wearing a yellow dress and sipping champagne."

"Sipping Champagne in a yellow dress at a society ball? Kate, I'm in mourning. I just told you about the harrowing experience of my survival, and you think that two months later I'd be enjoying festivities—two months after losing my beloved brother—the only family I have—" She shook her head, seemingly unable to continue. Tears pooled in her eyes, and she covered her mouth with her trembling hand.

Kate's stomach shriveled. What an awful, horrible friend she was. "I'm sorry! Of course, you weren't there. I was mistaken. I'm a fool. I don't know what I'm saying. Please forgive me!"

Emilia sniffed. "Sometimes, I'm so distraught that I imagine I see him, walking on the street or driving past me in a carriage. He'll appear out of nowhere—my darling brother—as real as if he stood before me in the flesh. But to be sure, it is only a figment of my imagination." She gave Kate a sad smile. "You mustn't think yourself mad. Grief can play powerful tricks on the mind. It happens to the best of us."

Kate nodded. Her certainty of what she'd thought she'd seen was now shattered. "Oh, Emilia, I have missed you. I don't think I realized just how much until this moment." She embraced her friend. Emilia was right. It had been her imagination. Emilia could not have been at Lady Ashworth's ball. She was in deep mourning for her brother.

Emilia wiped a tear from her eye. "I can't tell you how guilty I feel, knowing that I survived the accident and darling Theo perished," she said. "I wish he were the one sitting here with you now."

Kate reached for her friend's hand. "Oh, my dearest Emilia. How you must suffer."

"It's not only the pain of losing a brother—to be sure—that is agony. But now that Theo's gone, I've found myself completely destitute and alone in the world. I'm so afraid, Kate."

"You're not destitute. You have me. And you'll stay with us. We will introduce you to society, and I am sure you will make a wonderful match and have a family of your own one day. Our children will grow up together and be the best of friends."

"They'll be cousins," Emilia said, smiling through her tears. "To think you might be carrying a little Theo in your womb." She placed a hand on Kate's stomach, "It's so...I can't..." Emilia's lovely blue eyes turned watery again.

"Oh, Emilia. I miss him, too."

"Do you?" Emilia asked, her voice suddenly cold.

"Of course, I do," Kate protested, somewhat taken aback. "I loved Theo, you know that." But guilt gnawed at Kate as she spoke. Since marrying Oliver, she realized that she'd never truly loved Theo, not in the way she loved Oliver. Theo had assuaged her fears of being an old maid, left behind to rot as her father's keeper. He'd whispered sweet words telling her how beautiful she was and how much he desired her, but she'd never felt as connected to him as she did to Oliver. Oliver was her one true love, but she couldn't admit that to Emilia.

"I know you did," Emilia said, suddenly warm again. "I bore witness to your love. But when I look at this house and the handsome earl you married, I can't help wondering if, deep down, you are happy that things turned out the way they did. You're happy Theo is dead."

Kate's chest tightened as guilt took hold. "Emilia don't say such things! I am happy I met Oliver. He is my husband, and I love him dearly. But I loved Theo too. He is my child's father and will always have a special place in my heart."

Emilia smiled. "I'm sure he will. And I'm so pleased that I'll have the chance to tell his son or daughter all about him. It will be like having a part of him with me again."

Kate bit her lip. She'd have to have a difficult conversation with Emilia about the child, and she'd have to tread very carefully so as not to injure her further. "I am so pleased you will be part of your niece's or nephew's life. But you must remember, never mention that Oliver is not the child's father. If you do it will ruin his ability to inherit Oliver's title, or if it's a girl, her opportunity to make a good match. It's for the good of the child. You understand that don't you?"

For a minute, Kate thought she saw a coldness in Emilia's gaze, and her heart froze in fear. But then Emilia smiled, and the warmth in her eyes returned. "I understand," she said, leaning in to give Kate another embrace. "You can count on me being your greatest confidant and friend." She placed her hand on Kate's belly. "I already cherish this child. He's all I have left of my brother." Then she turned away, but before she did, Kate caught another glimpse of the frost in Emilia's eyes, and it sent a shiver down her spine. But she immediately pushed the feeling aside. Poor Emilia had suffered tremendously, while she'd been living a dream. Her dearest friend was right. She'd barely taken the time to mourn Theo. Instead, she'd selfishly indulged in a new happiness. So, who was she to judge Emilia?

Chapter Ten

A Week Later

"You look positively radiant," Oliver said, kissing his wife.

"Do I? Well, then, it is thanks to you for letting Emilia stay. I can't tell you how much joy it brings me to have my dear friend back."

"And I can't tell you how much joy it brings me to see you happy," Oliver said. "But do be cautious. People suffering from grief can be unpredictable in their moods. If Emilia sometimes seems"—he paused—"a little different from her old self, know that it's only part of the grieving process. And you can always count on me for help if you feel overwhelmed."

Kate nodded, somewhat relieved to hear Oliver's explanation. At times, Emilia seemed like an entirely different person, and it hurt. But then she'd return to her previous self, and Kate would chastise herself for being unkind. It was good to know that none of it was her fault.

"Now"—Oliver circled his arm around his wife—"how is the planning for the dinner party going?"

"Marvelous. I'm preparing the invitations, and Emilia and I will be visiting the modiste today to be fitted for some new dresses. I hope you don't mind, darling. But I can't help wanting to get her something new for when she enters half-mourning in a few weeks. I'm think a violet dress will do nicely."

"Of course, my dear. Go and enjoy yourselves. You both deserve a treat."

KATE AND EMILIA spent a full day at the modiste and then enjoyed tea at Gunter's in Berkeley Square. They ordered a pot of tea and an assortment of teacakes, scones with clotted cream, and fresh berries. The plum and lemon cakes were Kate's favorites, and she put one of each on her plate. Being with child had made her ravenous.

"I cannot wait to see you out of your full mourning clothes and in that violet dress." Kate dropped a lump of sugar in her tea. "And in the meantime, the new black dress we ordered for you will do nicely for the dinner party." She took a bite of her lemon cake, chewed, and swallowed. "That is delicious," she said, taking a bite of the plum cake.

Emilia had not touched her tea or any cakes on the table.

"Why aren't you eating?" Kate asked.

"How could I when I have to listen to talk about dinner parties, dresses, and cakes while my brother is not yet cold in his grave? I thought you said you loved him."

Kate swallowed and put down her fork. "I did—I do. You know that. But we talked about this. How Theo would want us both to be happy."

"Look at you," Emilia said in a furious whisper, pointing to Kate's pink empire dress and matching bonnet. "You didn't spend one day in black mourning clothes, did you?"

Tears pricked Kate's eyes. She had wanted to wear black, but her papa would have grown suspicious. After all, he hadn't known about her betrothal. And then, Aunt Jane had carted her off to London. And the only person who wore full black at the Lyon's Den was Mrs. Dove Lyon. But Kate did not want to tell Emilia about that. "I'm sorry," she said, remembering Oliver's warning about potentially unpredictable behavior. Emilia was grieving. It wasn't her fault that she couldn't control her emotions. "That was insensitive of me. I didn't mean to imply that entering half mourning was something to celebrate."

"And what of *your* mourning period," Emilia snarled in a low voice. "The one that doesn't seem to have existed." She pushed back her chair, stood up, and marched away, leaving her tea and cakes untouched.

Kate quickly followed, and they walked in silence to Park Lane. She felt wretched. How could she convince Emilia that she wasn't happier now than before Theo died when that wasn't the truth? She *was guilty* of loving Oliver more than Theo and of not wanting to go back in time and change anything. Most of all, she was guilty of being the happiest she'd ever been.

"I see the way you are with Oliver," Emilia said as they approached the lavish Knox mansion. "You love him more than you loved Theo. Or maybe it's his money and his grand home you love more. But Theo's dead, and you can't hurt him anymore. Now, I worry for his child. You'll love Oliver's children more than you'll love Theo's child."

"No, Emilia." Kate grabbed Emilia's arm and forced her to stop. "How can you say such things? I know you've suffered these past months, but you mustn't think so poorly of me. I can't stand it." Kate thought about telling Emilia that Oliver couldn't sire children but decided against it.

Emilia gave Kate an icy stare before pushing open the gate and walking toward the front door.

A heavy weight settled on Kate's shoulders and stayed with her throughout the day. Emilia seemed to change from joyful one minute to angry and resentful the next. Kate wanted to be understanding. Her friend had suffered a devastating loss, and having been in the carriage with Theo when he died made it all the more painful for her. Poor Emilia was alone in the world, and she wanted her to feel like she had a family now that Kate carried Theo's babe.

Guilt gnawed at Kate. The most painful part of Emilia's behavior was not her tirade, but her words, because they were true. In two short months, Kate had fallen in love with another man—and not just fallen in love—the love she'd bourn for Theo paled in comparison to her love for Oliver. And that made her blameworthy.

"I trust the two of you had an enjoyable day and ordered new dresses for the dinner party," Oliver said when the three were seated at the dinner table.

"I've decided to cancel," Kate said, glancing at Emilia.

"Cancel?" Emilia exclaimed. "Whatever for? I'm so looking forward to wearing my lovely purple dress. It will cheer me up to start wearing a spot of color again," she said brightly.

Kate blinked. "I thought you—"

"Theo just loved me in purple," Emilia said, cutting off Kate's words. "It will be a bit of cheer after suffering so much pain." She dabbed her eyes with the corner of her napkin.

"I thought—I mean—If you want then of course I won't cancel."

"No, it's best you do. I don't want you to go to any trouble on my behalf. You've been so down lately. I expect you're tired, and I wonder if my presence here is too much for you."

"There's no need to do everything yourself, Kate," Oliver said, "Have the servants arrange things. It's three weeks away. They have ample time."

"Yes, of course." Kate frowned, still trying to digest the sudden change in Emilia's attitude.

"Oh dear," Emilia said, "now you look cross. I'm so very sorry, I hate to be such a nuisance."

Kate jerked her head up to face Emilia. "What, no I—"

"Is all this upset really necessary?" Oliver interjected. "There's no need to worry. The servants will take care of everything."

"You're right, of course." A lump formed in Kate's throat. How had everything turned against her when she did her best to please Emilia? They'd been having such a wonderful time planning the party together when Emilia had turned on her out of nowhere, and now Oliver thought she was being unreasonable, too.

"Do you know, I feel rather exhausted," Kate said, "would you both excuse me? I'd like to go and lie down."

"Of course, my love," Oliver stood up and kissed her lightly on the forehead, "make sure you get some rest."

Kate forced a smile and excused herself from the room. As she walked out, she heard Julia say, "Do you know, I feel like playing a jolly tune on the pianoforte. Would you care to be my audience?"

"I'd love that. Thank you," Oliver replied.

Kate paused. Was it her imagination, or was Emilia only angry and upset when they were alone together? What in the world had gotten into her?

It was almost as though she blamed Kate for Theo's death.

Chapter Eleven

The following morning, Kate ran her hand across the bed sheets, feeling for her husband's warmth.

"Oliver," she murmured, still half asleep. "Oliver," she repeated, opening her eyes.

The bed was empty. Had she slept late? She had no recollection of Oliver coming to bed, but perhaps she'd been in a deep sleep. Kate reached for the small bell beside her bed and rang for her lady's maid.

"My lady, you're awake?" Elspeth said as she entered a few seconds later.

"Why? What time is it?"

"Past noon. You must have been exhausted, my lady."

"And where is Lord Knox?"

"In his study, my lady. He rose early and breakfasted with Miss Harrington. Then they went out for a ride together. He left instructions not to wake you."

"Oh," Kate said. "And where is Miss Harrington now?"

"Downstairs, preparing everything for the dinner party tonight."

"What?"

"The dinner party. Miss Harrington has given the servants a menu and a host of instructions. She said you're not to be disturbed."

Kate blinked. *But the dinner party is in three weeks. What on earth is going on?*

"Is everything quite all right, my lady?" Elspeth asked. "Shall I fetch you some tea?"

Kate shook her head. "I must have forgotten about the party. It's a good thing Miss Harrington has taken charge." Kate forced a smile, but a chill ran through her. Something wasn't quite right, she thought as she made her way downstairs. The trouble was, she didn't know if the problem was with her, or with Emilia, and there was no one who she could ask. Not after last night when Oliver seemed to be sympathetic to Emilia in spite of her odd behavior.

"Not over there. I want them on the table," Emilia instructed a footman, holding a vase of freshly cut flowers as Kate walked into the room. She wore a vibrant green dress that Kate recognized as one of her own.

"What are you doing?" Kate asked, coming up behind her.

Emilia spun around. "Oh, Kate, are you sure you should be up and about in your condition?"

"I'm fine." She eyed the green dress. "What happened to your mourning attire?"

"I took your advice. It's time to put the past behind me. Theo would have wanted me to be happy."

"I never said you should—" Kate began.

"Doesn't the room look fabulous?" Emilia spread out her arms. "I just love flowers."

"Yes, it looks marvelous. But why didn't you ask me before arranging a dinner party for tonight? I need to be ready to receive guests."

"Really, Kate. You said last night that if I wanted to go ahead with the dinner party, I could."

"I know that, but I didn't think it would be *tonight*. It's supposed to be three weeks from now."

"Oliver thinks it's a marvelous idea. And honestly, Kate, if it's too much for you, then Oliver and I will understand if you need to stay in bed."

Oliver and me? "Since when do you refer to my husband as—" Kate started when Emilia swooped forward and embraced her.

"Oh, Kate, darling, you are the greatest friend I will ever have. Organizing this dinner party has taken my mind off Theo and greatly reduced my suffering. I cannot thank you enough."

Kate's heart constricted as she melted into Emilia's embrace. She hated feeling suspicious of her friend. All she wanted was for Emilia to be happy.

"Come with me upstairs and help me find something pretty for tonight since my new dresses won't be ready for several days yet."

"I'd love to," Kate said. "But first, I need to visit Oliver in his study. We haven't seen each other since last night. And I need to have my tea. I missed breakfast this morning."

"Oh, I wouldn't disturb Oliver. He's been awfully busy this morning. And I am so excited to try on some dresses after wearing black for weeks on end. Let's have tea in my room. Then we can go to your dressing room and try on dresses the way we used to do in Yorkshire. It will be just like old times."

Kate smiled. Emilia's excitement was infectious. She supposed it would be best to let Oliver finish his work. She hated to disturb him in his study. Her stomach rumbled. "All right, you've convinced me," she said. "I'll request the tea to be brought to your room."

THEY SAT AT a small round table on armchairs upholstered in pale blue. A tea tray laden with cakes, scones, and fresh fruit awaited them.

Kate reached for the teapot.

"Let me." Emilia stood and picked up the teapot. She filled two cups and poured a dollop of cream in hers. You like sugar, don't you?" She dropped two lumps of sugar into Kate's tea and picked up a spoon, but it slipped from her fingers and landed on the soft white and blue rug beneath them.

"Oh, dear, I'm too clumsy today. Will you get that, Kate?"

"Of course," Kate bent to retrieve the spoon, and when she sat up, she glimpsed Emilia slipping something into her pocket.

"What's that?" She asked.

"What?" Emilia asked, handing Kate her tea.

"In your pocket. A little bottle."

"Oh, this." Emilia's cheeks flushed pink as she pulled a small glass vile from her pocket. "It's only a drop of lavender oil to calm my nerves, that's all." She sat down and drew her cup and saucer toward her. "It's been trying since the accident. I wasn't honest when I said I didn't have any injuries. My body has ached ever since, but not as much as my heart. A dash of lavender always helps."

"Oh, Emilia. I'm so sorry for you. You've been through such a terrible ordeal." Kate sipped her tea and frowned. It tasted wrong.

"I put a dash in yours too. I hope you don't mind. It smells divine, and it's so calming."

"I think it makes it rather bitter."

"Silly me! I forgot you liked your tea sweet." She stood and added two more lumps of sugar to Kate's teacup, before Kate could protest that Emilia had already put sugar in her tea before dropping the spoon. Then Emilia reached for a slice of sponge cake laden with marmalade and took a bite. "The cake looks delicious!" Kate's stomach rumbled furiously. "I'm ravenous," she giggled, forgetting all about her tea as she reached for a slice of plum cake.

After eating two slices of cake and one large scone, Kate took another sip of her tea and pulled a face. "This tea tastes awful. I must speak to the maidservant about this."

"Mine tastes perfectly fine," Emilia said. "You know, I once heard that being with child can change the way things taste to a woman. Perhaps that is the problem."

"I think you may be right. In these past few months, the smell of kippers makes me violently ill."

"Well, there you go! You've always loved kippers. Now drink your tea. It's good for you."

Kate forced down another gulp of tea but felt herself grow nauseous. She put down the cup and rested her hand on her still-slim stomach. "All that food has made me sleepy," she said, her eyelids suddenly feeling like two craters. It was impossible to keep them from closing.

"Here, you need to lie down. Let me help you." Emilia put an arm around Kate's waist, assisted her to stand, and then helped her walk to the bed.

Kate rested her head on the soft pillow as Emilia removed Kate's shoes and covered her with a blanket.

"Sweet dreams, dear Kate." Emilia's voice seemed to float past her ears before she drifted into the darkness.

OLIVER CLOSED HIS accounts book and fished his pocket watch from his jacket. It was close to three o'clock. He'd worked through tea after the butler informed him that his wife and Miss Harrington were taking tea together upstairs in the latter's room.

It pleased Oliver that Kate was feeling well enough to socialize with her friend. He'd been worried about her the night before. She'd seemed unusually perturbed and tired. He was concerned that she'd overexerted herself during her long day of shopping with Miss Harrington. And he was disturbed at how upset she'd seemed at the dinner table.

He'd decided that she'd needed rest, so he had slept in one of the spare bedrooms to ensure that Kate got a proper night's sleep, and it seemed to have worked. She'd slept right through the morning. But he'd missed the warmth of her body next to his during the night. He'd missed caressing her silky soft skin and her sweet floral scent. This morning, he'd missed waking up next to her, kissing her upon opening his eyes, and breakfasting with her before retreating to his study. Now it was afternoon, and he hadn't seen her since dinner yesterday. That was too long. Oliver pushed back his chair and stood up, smiling at the thought of holding Kate in his arms and taking in her scent. He needed to let her know how much he'd missed her last night.

"Kate," Oliver called as he pushed open the door to their bedchamber. His heart momentarily sank when he saw that Kate was not in sight but lifted again when he heard a rustling noise coming from Kate's adjoining dressing room. "Kate," he called, turning to walk into the large closet.

Then he stopped, shock and surprise momentarily paralyzing him.

Emilia stood in front of the oval full-length mirror, turning from side to side as she admired her reflection. She wore the royal blue gown Kate had worn to Lady Ashworth's ball. The ruby-encrusted diamond necklace that he'd given Kate as a wedding gift hung around her neck, and the matching earrings dangled from her earlobes.

"What are you doing?" Oliver said when he found his voice. "Where's Kate?"

Rather than turn around, she spoke to Oliver's reflection in the mirror, her ice-blue eyes fixing on his face. "What do you think?" She ran her hands down the sides of her hips. "Does it suit me?"

"It's far too small," Oliver said. His words were blunt, partly because he didn't like seeing her in Kate's clothing and partly because of the disappointment he felt upon seeing Emilia instead of his wife. "Where is Kate, and why are you wearing her clothes and jewelry?"

"She fell asleep in my bedroom as soon as tea was over," Emilia chuckled. "Poor thing, she's simply exhausted. She told me to help myself to anything in her wardrobe. My dresses won't be ready until next week." She turned to look at him and widened her blue eyes as if to plead her innocence. "You don't think I'd use Kate's things without her blessing, do you?"

"No, of course not." Oliver felt somewhat foolish. Emilia and Kate had been dear friends—almost sisters—long before he'd married Kate, so there was no need for him to overreact. And he imagined it was common for sisters to share clothing. Still, he couldn't rid himself of the feeling that something wasn't quite right as far as Emilia was concerned.

"Good," Emilia said, putting her hands on her hips and striding toward Oliver, "Now tell me, how do I look in this dress? Will it suffice for our dinner party tonight?"

Oliver frowned and took a step back. "What do you mean tonight? We're not having a dinner party tonight."

"Yes, we are. Remember the dinner party Kate arranged in my honor? She was so sorry about how she behaved yesterday that she insisted we have the party tonight. However, she was too fatigued to make the arrangements, so I had to take over. It's unfortunate, but I don't think she'll be able to attend. She's far too exhausted. Carrying a babe uses all of a woman's energy."

"I'm sorry to disappoint you, Miss Harrington, but I'm not throwing a dinner party if my wife is unable to attend."

"But the invitations have already been sent out."

"Then I will send my messenger to deliver cancellation and apology notices to all invitees."

"If you prefer a quiet night at home," Emilia said, inching closer, "then we can have one together—just the two of us."

"What?" Oliver took a step back.

"Oh, Oliver, you don't need to put on a brave stance with me. I know how difficult it must be for you—a newly married man—forced to sleep separate from his wife because she's carrying another man's child. But you needn't spend any nights alone while Kate is with child because I am always here for you."

"That's enough, Miss Harrington!" Oliver said. "I'd like you to take off Kate's clothing and jewelry. I think it's time I arranged alternative accommodations for you."

Emilia snorted. "You jest! I'm offering you a gift that no man would turn down. Kate never need know anything about it."

"I'm sorry to disappoint you, but your offer holds no interest for me. Now, if you'll excuse me, I'm going to find my wife."

Emilia's face hardened, and her eyes turned glacial. "Go ahead. She's in my chamber, dead to the world."

The hair on the nape of Oliver's neck stood on end. Emilia was dangerous. Why hadn't he seen it before? He turned and strode out of the bedchamber. He needed to find Kate immediately.

CHAPTER TWELVE

OLIVER RACED DOWN the hallway to the guest chamber where Emilia was staying. True to Emilia's word, Kate lay fast asleep on her bed. He breathed a sigh of relief as he walked over to her and stroked her hair lovingly. A smile formed on her lips in response to his touch, though she did not wake. Oliver bent to kiss her forehead and then turned to leave. But paused when the tea tray caught his eye. Remnants of half-eaten teacakes and two teacups with shallow pools of cold tea left behind sat on the table. But the tea in one of the teacups had an unusual dark reddish hue. He picked up the cup, tilting it forward to reveal powdered sediments at the bottom. Smelling the contents, he recoiled.

The strong smell of laudanum mixed with lavender filled his nostrils. Gingerly, he tasted the tea. As soon as the cold liquid touched his tongue, he winced at its bitterness. The tea had been tainted with a large amount of laudanum powder and masked with sugar and lavender. How could Kate not have noticed?

He turned to his sleeping wife. He had to get her out of Emilia's room and send for the doctor immediately. Oliver rang the servant's bell and paced the room until Elspeth appeared.

"My lord!" she said, startled to see him in Emilia's room.

"I need you to send for the doctor at once," he said, gently lifting Kate in his arms. "Direct him to Lady Knox's bedchamber when he arrives."

Elspeth gasped. "Is my lady ill, my lord?"

"Just do as I ask, Elspeth. Hurry."

Elspeth reached for the tea tray.

"Leave it!" Oliver said.

Elspeth nodded and hurried down the corridor, and Oliver carried Kate back to their bedchamber, setting her down on the bed just as Emilia came out of the dressing room, after having changed back into her own dress.

"You gave her laudanum," Oliver barked, "that's why she's fast asleep."

"Only to help her get the rest she needs," Emilia said. "Laudanum won't do her or the babe any harm."

"Not in small amounts but you gave her too much. I saw remnants of the powder in the cup. How dare you administer medication to my wife? You're not a doctor."

"Oh please, mothers give laudanum to ease their children's ailments all the time. Even infants are given laudanum. It can't do her any harm."

"That's not the point!" Oliver ran a hand through his hair. Losing his temper wasn't going to help Kate. "I want you to leave this house."

"You will throw me on the street? Your own cousin."

"I would if it weren't for Kate." He reached into his pocket and pulled out a banknote. "But seeing as she loves you, I will have my driver escort you to an inn until I can find you suitable employment of some type."

"Employment?" She spat out the word as if it were poison.

"Yes, as a companion to an elderly lady or some such respectable job that will give you food and shelter."

"I think you are mistaken, my lord," she said, snatching the banknote. "I don't want your charity. I want my own house and a fortune to go with it."

"I realize you have been through a very traumatic experience, but I hardly think it wise for you to come into my home and make demands, Miss Harrington. Do not presume to take advantage of my generosity."

"I think you misunderstand our positions."

"How so?" Oliver clasped his hands together to keep himself from reaching out to the woman. He wanted to grasp her by the shoulders and shake her.

"You seem to be forgetting that I know that Kate's babe is not yours."

Oliver narrowed his eyes. "You would ruin the life of your deceased brother's child?"

She smirked. "My brother was a fool. He allowed Kate to trick him and seduce him."

"So, you want me to pay you in exchange for your silence," Oliver said through gritted teeth.

"Exactly. Fund the lifestyle I want, and this will all go away. No one will know your child is illegitimate."

"I would have taken care of you, let you live with us, and have food and clothing without question. But that wasn't enough for you," he growled. "You threaten blackmail. But I'll have you know—no one will believe you," Oliver said. "I am an earl and Kate is my wife. You can't prove anything."

"They will believe me. Why else would your wife have auctioned herself off for marriage at a notorious gaming den? Only a woman in dire circumstances would do such a thing."

Oliver's felt the blood drain from his face. "How do you know that?" He froze, a sudden memory of Lady Ashworth's ball coming into his mind. *That is where I saw her—at the ball, standing next to*

Middlemarch. That snake Middlemarch will rue the day he crossed me and the Black Widow of Whitehall.

"I want you out of my house!" Oliver snapped.

"Indeed," she said, folding the banknote into the bosom of her dress. "And you needn't bother with an escort, I will call a hansom to take me to a friend's house. I'm not staying at an inn like some commoner."

"A friend? I wasn't aware you had any friends in London. Except, now that I think about it without friends in high places, how on earth did you get an invitation to Lady Ashworth's ball? Could you have been the guest on Lord Middlemarch, perhaps?"

Emilia's lips curled into a pernicious smile. "As long as you keep paying me, your dear Kate won't have anything to worry about. But if you fail to cooperate, all of London will hear about the Earl of Knox's soon-to-be bastard."

"She's breathing normally and her heart sounds strong. She's not in any distress, so I think there is no harm done. As long as it was only laudanum. Did you check the cup?"

"Yes, I tasted the contents. It was laudanum, and quite a lot of it."

"In that case I wouldn't worry. She'll likely sleep through the night and wake up feeling refreshed tomorrow. But if you're concerned, have someone sit with her and monitor her breathing."

"Thank you, Doctor. And what about the babe, does all look well?"

"All is fine. The child will likely get a good night's rest too."

Oliver nodded. He felt somewhat foolish for panicking over laudanum, but seeing Kate on that bed in Emilia's room sent him back to a darker time—a time he didn't care to relive. He bid the doctor goodbye and sat with Kate for a few minutes before kissing her lightly on the forehead and going downstairs. He instructed his servants to cease preparing for the dinner party immediately and sent Kate's lady's maid upstairs to sit with her until she awoke. After sending out a messenger with the appropriate cancellation and apology messages to his dinner guests, he had a word with his butler.

"I need to go out and tend to some urgent business. See to it that Miss Harrington's bags are packed and that she leaves this house before my return. Elspeth must remain with Kate until Miss Harrington has left the premises, do you understand?"

"Yes, my lord. I'll see to it myself."

"Excellent," Oliver said.

Five minutes later, he climbed into his black and gold carriage, bearing his family crest.

"Where to, my lord?" The footman asked before closing the carriage door.

"Cleveland Street." Oliver sat back in the buttoned leather seat. "The Lyon's Den."

THE MORNING FOLLOWING Lord Knox's visit to her office, Bessie Dove-Lyon crossed St. James's Street and entered the white three-story building that was home to Boon's Gentleman's Club.

"Hello, Baxter. How are you today?" she greeted the doorman as she entered. "I'm here to see Mr. Boon. Is he in his office?"

"He is, Mrs. Dove-Lyon. I'll escort you upstairs."

"Never mind, don't bother leaving your post. I know the way."

He nodded and she made her way up the stairs to the first floor of the building. Since it was before noon, the gaming rooms were not yet open, and the building was calm and silent, which was quite a different atmosphere from what it would be like a few hours from now. The rooms would be filled with smoke and gentlemen gambling—some increasing and some losing their livelihoods.

She approached Henry Boon's office door where another doorman stood. "Good morning, Six," she said. "I'm here to see Mr. Boon."

"Certainly, Mrs. Dove-Lyon. Mr. Boon always has time for you." He rapped on the door with his knuckles and then pushed it open. "Mrs. Dove-Lyon is here to see you, sir."

"Is she, indeed?" Bessie heard Henry Boon's unmistakable throaty voice. "Well, send her inside."

Six held the door open for Bessie and then closed it behind her as she stepped into Henry Boon's lavish office. He stood to greet her. He was a short, portly man, with a bulbous nose and face full of scars that looked like the result of a childhood pox.

"Do take a seat Mrs. Dove-Lyon." She sat on a chair across from his desk as he settled back in his chair and clasped his hands together. "Tell me, to what do I owe this honor?" he asked.

"I have a thorn in my side that needs extracting," Bessie said.

Boon raised his eyebrows. "And you cannot extract this thorn on your own?"

"Unfortunately, he's been banned from my club and so is out of my reach."

"Mmm. And does this irritant have a name?"

"Middlemarch. Lord Maximus Middlemarch. I believe he's been frequenting your establishment since I banned him from my club."

Boon stroked his chin. "A peer. I see."

"He's a baron. Will that be a problem?"

"Is his estate entailed?"

"Yes. But if you leave him with nothing else but that which will eventually amount to a crumbling ruin in Kent, then I will consider the job done."

Boon nodded. "This could be a dangerous operation. Cheating is a serious offense. If anyone got a whiff of that, my place could be closed down."

"That won't happen. I have magistrates and plenty other powerful men who are indebted to me, so if anything goes wrong—and I am assuming nothing will go wrong because you are an expert at what you do—the allegations will be swiftly quashed."

Boon inclined his head. "Still, the risk is all mine, so I'll want seventy percent of the proceeds."

"We'll do a fifty-fifty split," Bessie said firmly.

Henry shifted in his seat.

"If this doesn't suit, I can always pay a visit to Riley's just up the street. I'm sure John Riley will—"

"No, no!" Boon sighed. "You drive a hard bargain, Mrs. Dove-Lyon, but considering our long history of helping each other, I will take a fifty-fifty split."

"Excellent," Bessie said, "let's say tomorrow evening you lure Middlemarch into your club with an invitation-only poker game—sent exclusively to your most esteemed clients and best players—something his ego won't allow him to resist."

"Aah, excellent idea, playing to the man's vanity. And once he's committed to the game, I'll put my man Six across from him. He's a savant at counting cards."

Bessie nodded. She knew all about Six. When Boon had first caught him counting cards in his establishment, he threatened to cripple the man's hands, but Six quickly offered up his services and has been faithful to Boon ever since.

"Success is guaranteed, then?" Bessie said.

"With Six, yes."

"And how will you ensure that Middlemarch keeps gambling? Will free-flowing brandy and whiskey be enough to do the trick?"

"That and a little of this." He opened his drawer and extracted a small bottle from his desk.

"What is that?"

"Just a little tincture to inject an extra bit of energy. Only the minutest drop in a glass of brandy is needed to do the trick. It will keep him playing for hours. He will feel as though he is on top of the world even when he is losing his britches."

"Outstanding," Bessie said. "I knew I could count on you, Boon." She stood up.

"Tell me, what did the unfortunate fellow do to you?" Boon asked.

"He breached confidentiality. No one comes to the Lyon's Den and gossips about what they saw or heard there—no one. Not unless they want to suffer the consequences, that is."

Boon looked at the veiled woman with admiration and nodded. "It's a pleasure doing business with you, Mrs. Dove-Lyon. A real pleasure," he said. "And you can count on me to get the job done."

"I know I can," Bessie said. "But everyone will know I was behind it, and my message will come across loud and clear. If you cross Bessie Dove-Lyon, you will pay a heavy price."

Bessie exited Boise's gentleman's club with a sense of satisfaction, but her job was not yet done. Now it was time to visit some of her oldest friends.

Chapter Thirteen

"I don't understand any of this." Kate sat beside Oliver on the ornate scarlet sofa in Mrs. Dove-Lyon's office. "Emilia is my dearest friend. How could she turn against me? If I can just talk to her, I'm sure she'll explain."

"How long did you know her in Yorkshire?" Oliver asked.

Kate bit her lip. The truth was she'd only known Emilia for seven or eight months. But she'd been so desperate for friends her age and Emilia had been such wonderful company that they'd become instant best friends. And when Emilia had introduced Kate to Theo, her world changed. Finally, she'd met a man—a handsome, kind man—who'd loved her and wanted to marry her. Emilia and Theo had given her a new family.

"Perhaps Middlemarch influenced her thinking?" Kate said, ignoring Oliver's question. "Where on Earth could she have met him?"

"I don't know, but I suspect that is why Mrs. Dove-Lyon called us here today She has far-reaching connections, that's why I asked for her help in this matter."

"Is that how Middlemarch came to ruin?"

"I imagine she had something to do with it, yes. Don't tell me you pity him."

"No," Kate shook her head. "He got what he deserved."

"Lord and Lady Knox," the Black Widow of Whitehall entered the room, wearing her signature black dress and veil that obscured her features. She sat across from Kate and Oliver on one of her plush, scarlet armchairs. A maidservant entered seconds later and placed a silver tea tray on the oval table at the center of the seating area.

"I have done a little sleuthing on our behalf, and I must say I enjoyed it very much," Mrs. Dove-Lyon said.

"Did you manage to uncover anything about Miss Harrington?" Oliver asked.

"Indeed. It seems Miss Harrington, as she is known to you, used to go by the name Fanny Birch."

Kate inhaled sharply. "What? Do you mean she's not Theo's sister?"

"That's correct. She was born in St. Giles where she worked as a courtesan for a few years. She was popular because of her beauty, and it wasn't long before a man took her away with him to the continent, but that relationship didn't last, and she soon found herself destitute in France. There she took up her profession again. And that is where she met your cousin, Mathew Harrington, whom she called 'Theo'."

Kate's mind whirled as she tried to digest Mrs. Dove-Lyon's words. She had thought Emilia was her best friend but, it turned out, she'd been a complete stranger. Worse, she didn't know the man with whom she'd fallen in love. Instead, she'd trusted them both, given them her heart and even her body. What a fool she'd been! "Are you saying that Mathew and Emilia were lovers?"

"Precisely."

Kate put her trembling hand over her mouth to stifle her gasp. She shook her head. *It's impossible. All those months the three of us spent together. There was no indication—or perhaps, I was too naive to notice. Dear Lord, how is this possible?* Suddenly, it felt as though the world was about to open up under Kate's feet. She swayed in her chair.

Oliver reached for Kate's hand, and she seized it. The world immediately righted itself. He was her rock, her solid ground, and her safe place. He'd take care of her, always. She had no doubts about him, and she never would.

"But why did they pretend to be siblings? And why did Emilia introduce me to Theo—Mathew—and encourage our relationship?" Kate managed to say.

"For money, my dear. They didn't have any, so Mathew needed to marry a woman whose father *did* have money—someone like you. And if you believed that Emilia was his sister and loved her as one too, she would have been able to live with the two of you. I suspect Mathew would have found excuses to stay away from your bed over time. And the less time he spent in your bed, the more he would have spent in hers. It's not such an uncommon scheme, I'm afraid."

Kate's eyes filled with tears. She hadn't wanted to believe the horrible things Oliver had told her about Emilia. She was sure there'd be a rational explanation. But now there was no denying it. Theo and Emilia had used her. And, worst of all, she'd been gullible enough to give herself away to a man who'd had no love for her.

"What an utter fool I've been." She buried her face in Oliver's chest as he put a comforting arm around her shoulders and pulled her toward him.

"Don't be so hard on yourself," Mrs. Dove Lyon said. "There's more to this story." She paused to pour a cup of tea and Kate steeled herself for more bad news.

"I suspect things didn't go as planned for Emilia." The widow picked up her cup. "You see, Mathew wasn't as disingenuous as you think. Although he initially planned to deceive you into marrying him, he later fell in love with you. And when you told him about the child, he proposed in earnest. This, of course, enraged Emilia—so much so, that she came up with a scheme to murder him."

"Murder!" Kate jerked her head up. "How?"

"By causing the carriage accident that led to his death."

"I—I can hardly believe what I'm hearing. Emilia was in the carriage with him. She could have died when the carriage overturned."

"I don't believe Emilia was in the carriage at the time of the accident," Mrs. Dove Lyon said. "The story she told about surviving the accident and being taken in by a farmer and his wife sounded preposterous, at least to me. I made some inquiries, but no one has been able to locate this phantom couple. I propose they don't exist. And when Lord Knox told me how Emilia put laudanum in your tea, a thought came to my mind. I believe she did the same to Mathew Harrington, giving him a flask of brandy laced with laudanum to enjoy on his journey—the drug would have caused him to become drowsy, resulting in a fatal accident."

"Good Lord," Oliver whispered, still clutching Kate's trembling hand.

"Of course, this is only my theory. We need proof," Mrs. Dove-Lyon said.

"How can we prove it?" Kate asked.

"We can't, so you'll need to pry the truth out of Emilia. I suggest you invite her for tea. Send her a note, telling her you miss her, and that you want to hear her side of the story. She's bound to take the opportunity to try and sway you to her side and turn you against your husband, so I am convinced she'll accept your invitation. Once you sit down with her, you will put my theory to her, which will enrage her and cause her to throw caution to the wind. When she realizes that she cannot sway you and has lost her control over you, she will want to punish you. And what better way does she have of hurting you by admitting to the truth? She'll no doubt want to brag about how she outwitted you and Oliver. But what she won't know is that Lord Knox and Magistrate Thomas will be in the next room, listening to her every word."

"Magistrate Thomas?" Oliver said. "Can he be trusted to keep our secret?"

The widow put down her cup and, Kate was sure, fixed a stern gaze on Oliver from beneath her veil. "He's a loyal patron and can be trusted to keep private, sensitive information out of the official report after Emilia is arrested for murder. He won't breathe a word about your child's legitimacy, nor will he give Emilia the chance to do so, that I can promise you."

"SHE'S ON HER way up," Olive said. "Are you sure you want to do this?"

Kate nodded. "I've never been more certain about anything in my life. I need to know the truth. And if Emilia is guilty, she should pay for her crimes."

"Very well, then. But remember, Magistrate Thomas and I will be in the adjoining room. We'll be able to hear every word you say, and if she becomes threatening toward you, we will be by your side in a matter of seconds."

Kate straightened her shoulders. "I'm ready."

Oliver kissed her and then left to join the magistrate in the neighboring room.

Seconds later, the butler opened the door to the drawing room and announced, "Miss Emilia Harrington to see Lady Knox."

"Emilia, come in." Kate worked hard to sound cheerful and welcoming as she opened her arms to her former friend though her stomach felt sour with disgust. "I'm so pleased you agreed to see me."

"And I am so pleased you invited me to talk." Emilia embraced Kate. "I thought you'd abandoned me."

"Never." Kate gestured for the woman to sit down. Then she sat across from her and poured her a cup of tea, adding a lump of sugar and a dollop of cream before handing it to her. "I would never abandon you, my dear sister." *Nor would I add laudanum to your cup, though honestly, it would serve you right.* Kate pushed the thought away. Now was not the time to let her temper get the better of her, even if her ire was well deserved.

"Thank you." Emilia smiled sweetly and sipped her tea.

"But I do have a few questions for you," Kate said. "And I need you to answer me honestly."

"Or course."

"I believe it was Middlemarch who tried to turn you against me and Oliver." She sipped her tea. "None of this is your fault. He is the guilty party. Where did you meet him?"

"After Theo's death, I found Lord Knox's letter, naming Mathew—Theo—as his heir, so I came to London in search of him in the hope that he would help the unprotected sister of his deceased heir. I stayed a few nights at an inn in London, and when I went down for dinner one evening, I met Middlemarch. He was drinking and gambling, and when he spotted me alone, he came to talk to me." Emilia tilted her chin in what Kate knew was false modesty, especially given the woman's true character. "He wanted to know why such a beautiful and respectable lady was dining alone. I knew he was a gentleman, so I allowed him to dine with me. I thought he might know Lord Knox, so I told him I was a relative of the earls. And that is when he invited me to Lady Ashworth's ball."

"But why didn't you approach me when I saw you at the party? You denied being there. I thought I was going mad." Again, Kate pushed away the anger boiling in her belly as she remembered the angst she'd endured at the wicked woman's hand. Remembering that Oliver and the magistrate were listening helped. If she lost her temper, they'd never get the information they needed to make Emilia—

Fanny—pay for her crimes.

"I was shocked. I didn't expect to see you there. Middlemarch had mentioned that Lord Knox was recently married, but I had no idea it was you. I wasn't ready to face you yet, so I turned and ran away."

"I don't believe you," Kate said. *Now. Now is the time. But tread carefully.* It occurred to Kate that this woman was adept at scheming and weaving webs to ensnare her victims; now it was her turn.

She reminded herself that the Black Widow, ironically, was on her side, and always had been. Kate didn't want to let her down. Certainly, she could weave a few traps of her own. But first, she needed to draw Fanny out into the light. "I wish you'd stop lying to me."

Emilia's eyes flashed with anger. "I'm not lying."

Kate set her cup down. *Be calm. Don't allow her to escape.* "I know that Theo wasn't your brother, Emilia." She kept her voice level and serene, even to her own ears. She wasn't going to give anything away.

Emilia blanched. "What? That's a lie. Where did you hear that?"

"From Theo," Kate said, intentionally meeting the woman's cold eyes with a stony gaze of her own.

"Liar!" Emilia said through gritted teeth.

Kate shrugged and waved her hand dismissively. "He told me everything before he died. He said that your real name is Fanny Birch and that he met you in a brothel in Paris. He loved you once—or he thought he did. Until he met me, of course." Kate found it easier to lie to Emilia—rather, *Fanny*—than she'd thought. She was glad to see the woman's facade crumble, and she wondered if Fanny had enjoyed seeing her fall apart as well. It gave her strength to keep baiting her.

But Fanny only laughed. "You're lying. Theo didn't tell you any of that, even though every word of it is true."

So she admits it and doesn't deny it. Kate felt a flush of success. She raised a brow. "What do you mean?" Kate asked. "How do you *know* he didn't tell me?"

"Because I have the letter he wrote you."

"What letter?" Kate cocked her head.

"The one he never had a chance to send you. Theo wrote to you confessing everything you just told me." She reached into her reticule and pulled out a crumpled envelope. "I found it, and that's when I decided he needed to die."

Kate reached for the letter, but Fanny held it back out of her grasp. "He wasn't supposed to fall in love with you!" A flash of fury appeared in her icy blue eyes. "That wasn't part of the plan!"

"What plan?" Kate asked.

"The plan to get your father's money, you little idiot. It was perfect. I knew from the day I met you—a desperate, lonely young woman who thought she'd die an old maid serving her father—you would have fallen in love with the first man who showed you an ounce of attention."

Kate flinched. It was true. She'd admitted it to herself already, but that didn't mean Fanny's verbal jab missed its mark. She drew herself up. *Calm, Kate. Be calm and think of Mrs. Dove-Lyon. She'd never allow herself to crumble when she was working on a snare.*

Perhaps that's why she always wore her veil, Kate realized. If no one could see her face, she didn't have to work at keeping her expression emotionless. It was more difficult than she'd thought it would be.

"And my Theo, well, he was handsome and charming. I knew it wouldn't take much for him to convince you to lie with him. Once you were with child, your father would have had no choice but to let you marry, and he'd have had to hand over a large dowry for the sake of his family's reputation. You'd have been Mrs. Harrington in name only—that was the plan. We'd have your money and each other." Fanny's lips curled in a snarl. "But after a while, I saw his attitude toward you change. Suddenly, he talked about having a proper marriage with you and leaving *me* out in the cold. He'd talk about your little family, and I knew he wanted me gone, so I devised a little plan of my own."

Kate's stomach turned. She thought of Middlemarch's pride, even to his own detriment. He and this woman were birds of a feather. Like him, Fanny would preen herself under praise, and even boast of what she no doubt saw as her accomplishments no matter how evil they were. So Kate tipped her head as if she admired Fanny's inventiveness. "You weren't with him in the carriage when it crashed down the ravine, were you?"

Fanny shook her head, a smile appearing on her face. "No."

"So what did you do? Lace his tea with laudanum as you did mine?"

"Not tea," she said, still smiling. "It's too weak to mask the bitterness of laudanum. You complained your tea was bitter, remember? I had to add four lumps of sugar and that still wasn't enough." She paused. "But for him, it was simple. I gave him a flask of brandy laced with laudanum. It masked the color of the drug and was strong enough to mask the taste. He drank it and dozed off, which caused his carriage to veer off the road."

Kate's eyes burned with tears. *There.* The confession she'd sought hung in the air. She didn't have to pretend anymore or hide her true feelings. "You're evil."

"He was going to leave me—marry you and kick me out like a dog—after all we'd been through." She held up the letter. "I suspected he'd been keeping something from me, so I searched his bags, and I found two letters—one from Lord Knox to Theo and another addressed to you." She held the letter out to Kate, almost tauntingly.

Kate snatched it from the woman's grip. Surprisingly, Fanny allowed her to unfold it and begin reading silently.

Her head swam. It was all there. The letter confirmed everything Emilia had said. Theo had confessed the truth and pledged his love for her and their child. He intended to talk to her father as soon as he returned from his trip to London, where he was going to meet his sixth cousin, the Earl of Knox.

When your Papa learns that I am to inherit an earldom, he will surely not refuse to let us marry. All will be well in a few days, my love. One day, you will be Lady Knox, the wife of a future earl who adores you.

Yours truly for life,
Theo

A tear leaked from Kate's eye and rolled down her cheek.

"Don't cry for him. He doesn't deserve tears. He thought he was clever, but I was cleverer. I killed him and got away with it," Fanny boasted. "And now, I'll kill you and no one will know. I'll tell Oliver you fell down or fell asleep and never woke up. I haven't decided yet." She grinned, her eyes glittering insanely. "And I'll be here to lift his spirits, and then—in time—*I'll* become his wife."

"No, you won't." Both Kate and Emilia turned to see Oliver standing in the doorway with that magistrate. His eyes were fiery as he glared at Kate's former friend. Or tormentor. At this point, Kate wasn't sure.

"Oliver!" She leapt to her feet and ran to her husband, longing more than ever for his protective embrace.

"Fanny Birch"—the magistrate strode forward—"you are under arrest for the murder of Mathew James Harrington." He gripped her by the arm and bodily dragged her to her feet.

Fanny struggled. Her eyes softened, and her tone was wheedling, almost shrill. "No, please. Kate, help me! Don't let them take me. I beg you! We're *sisters!*"

"We were never sisters. I know that now. Would that I had realized it when we first met," Kate said, looking directly into Emilia's cold blue eyes. Then she turned to the magistrate. "Get her out of my house. This woman is a liar and a murderer. I never want to see her again."

The magistrate dragged Fanny away and though they could still hear her protesting shrieks, a peace fell over the room. Oliver drew Kate to him. "Well done, my love. I must confess, I was a bundle of nerves, ready to spring into the drawing room and save you at any moment. But you didn't need saving. You stayed calm in the face of her anger and tricked her into confessing. Even Magistrate Thomas was impressed."

"I never want to have to do anything like that again." Kate buried her head in his chest and breathed her relief as he wrapped his arms tightly around her. It felt as though the weight of an elephant had been lifted off her back.

"And you won't have to. It's all over now." Oliver stroked her hair. "You were so brave. You got justice for Theo. And now, he can rest in peace."

Chapter Fourteen

Seven Months Later

OLIVER PACED OUTSIDE the bedchamber, his heart pounding as he heard his wife's screams. "It's perfectly normal for birthing women to scream, the doctor had told him. It's a painful process, but she won't remember the pain once it's over. All she will remember is the midwife placing her beautiful son or daughter in her arms."

Oliver kept reminding himself of these words, hoping they would ease his fears. He wanted to rush into the room and save Kate from whatever horror she was experiencing, but all he could do was pray. For the second time in his life, he felt completely powerless. The first had been when Beatrice had fallen ill, and he could do nothing to save her. And now that same helplessness overwhelmed him.

Finally, the screams stopped, and all was silent.

Oliver ceased pacing. *What's happening? Why has everything gone silent?*

He could take no more. He had to go inside and get answers. As Oliver pushed open the bedchamber door, an animal-like cry sounded, followed by his wife's wail. "No more! Please, I'm exhausted."

"What's going on?" Oliver rushed inside, unable to see Kate, whose canopied bed was curtained off.

The midwife turned; her eyes wide with shock at seeing him enter the sacred birthing space. Oliver's gaze fell on the little bundle in her arms. He blinked, so mesmerized he was unable to move.

"Make haste," the doctor ordered from behind the canopy. There's another one coming."

"Another?" Oliver's heart raced. *Two babes?*

The midwife stepped forward and handed the bundle to Oliver. "Your daughter." She smiled and then raced to the doctor's side.

Oliver peered down at the tiny, scrunched face, and his heart swelled.

"My beauty," he whispered just as another wail sounded.

Soon, the midwife emerged with a second bundle.

"It's a boy!" she said.

Oliver thought he might explode with happiness. "And my wife? How is Lady Knox?"

"Excellent, my lord." The doctor emerged from behind the canopied bed, wiping his hands on a cloth.

Oliver made his way to his wife with their daughter in his arms. The midwife followed, carrying their son. Kate lay with her head resting against a mass of pillows. Her chestnut hair was matted with sweat and stuck to her forehead. But her smile was radiant, and Oliver had never seen her look more beautiful.

"Your son, my lady." The midwife handed the baby to Kate. Oliver sat beside her on the bed, still cradling his daughter.

"Two babes—a son and a daughter. Who knew we could be so lucky?" Oliver kissed Kate's damp forehead.

"I want to call her Olivia," Kate said, looking at the baby in Oliver's arms, after her Papa."

"I think that's perfect. And this little angel shall be Theo." Oliver smiled at his son, resting in Kate's arms.

"Oh, Oliver," Kate leaned against his shoulder, "I'm so happy."

"We're so happy. And we will be." Oliver gazed at the sweet faces of his newborn babes and saw a lifetime of love, laughter, and happiness before him. "Always."

Historical Note

When I first got the idea for this book, I was uncertain whether doctors knew or understood much about male infertility in the early 1800s. My research soon brought me to an article titled, "'They Are Called Imperfect Men,' Male Infertility and Sexual Health in Early Modern England" by Jennifer Evans, published in the *Social History of Medicine*, which indicates that they did. One fascinating historical tidbit I learned from this article was that some early surgeons used the term "imperfect men" to describe infertile males. Specifically, Evans quotes from a seventeenth-century medical book called *A Golden Practice of Physick* in which the authors Felix Platter, Abdiah Cole, and Nich. Culpepper note the use of this label for barren men.

Hence my title, *The Imperfect Lyon*.

About the Author

Aviva holds a master's degree in English and has a keen interest in British literature. She is an anglophile and Brontë enthusiast who is happiest when traveling to or writing about England. Inspiration for her first book, The Mist on Brontë Moor, came after she visited the Brontë Parsonage in Haworth.

Born and raised in Cape Town, South Africa, Aviva now lives in Southern California with her husband, two daughters, and rambunctious Yorkshire terrier—named for the oft-forgotten Brontë brother Branwell.

Website: www.avivaorrauthor.com
Twitter: twitter.com/aviva_orr
Facebook: facebook.com/AuthorAvivaOrr
Goodreads: goodreads.com/author/show/6464067.Aviva_Orr
Bookbub: bookbub.com/profile/aviva-orr

Printed in Great Britain
by Amazon